Haunted Park

 Published by Grosset & Dunlap, a division of Penguin Young Readers Group, 345 Hudson Street, New York, NY 10014. GROSSET & DUNLAP is a trademark of Penguin Group (USA) Inc. Published simultaneously in Canada. Printed in the U.S.A. Library of Congress Control Number: 2003103320

ISBN 0-448-43130-0 A B C D E F G H I J

by Katherine Noll
Cover illustration by Neil Stewart

Grosset & Dunlap • New York

• • • • • • • • •

"Jake! Watch out!"

Jake Jagger looked up from his lunch and saw a wadded-up napkin flying right toward his head. He ducked, but was too late. The napkin landed in his spiky blond hair.

"Carlos!" Jake barked. The dark-haired boy grinned at him.

"Sorry, Jake," Carlos said. "I thought I had a hole in one." He gestured toward the trash can behind Jake.

Jake pulled the napkin from his hair. He was new at Riverside Middle School. When Jake moved to Riverside, his next-door neighbor happened to be Carlos Vega. The boys quickly became friends.

"Gross, ketchup," Jake said. "I sure wish you were a better shot, Carlos."

"Well, you should have been paying more attention," Carlos said. He sat down next to Jake. "You looked totally lost in thought."

"It's Cliff Top Coasters," Jake said. "I've been trying to find a way to keep it from going out of business!"

"I still can't believe your brother George actually owns his own amusement park," Carlos said. "That is so cool!"

“It won’t be cool if he has to close it down,” Jake said glumly.

Just then, a group of kids walked by. The tall one in the center of the group pointed toward Jake.

“Oooooooo,” the boy moaned in an eerie voice. “It’s the ghost of Cliff Top Coasters.”

“Shut up, Derek,” Carlos retorted. “Leave Jake alone.”

“I wish Jake and his brother had left Cliff Top Coasters alone,” Derek said. “Ever since George took over, strange things have been going on in that park.”

A stocky boy in a Riverside Raiders jacket chimed in. “Yeah,” he said. “When Mr. Snoggle owned Cliff Top, no one heard screams coming from the park in the middle of the night!”

“My mother said she heard the rides were running by themselves at night,” a girl with a long brown ponytail said. “She won’t let me go to the park anymore. She thinks it’s not safe.”

“And at night you can see weird flashing lights,” Derek said. “I’ve seen them with my own eyes.”

“The park is not haunted!” Jake yelled.

Derek smirked. “Okay, Flaky Jakey. Whatever you say.” He walked away and the other kids followed him, laughing.

“He makes me so mad!” Jake said. He stood up

• • • • • • • • • •

and threw his lunch into the trash can. He had lost his appetite.

Jake sat back down. A loud *"phhhht"* noise filled the air. Jake jumped up, red-faced. He looked down and saw a deflated whoopee cushion on his seat.

"Hanna!" Jake cried.

A giggling, red-haired girl leaped out from behind a chair.

"Hi, Jake," Hanna said, laughing. "Is the cafeteria food giving you gas?"

"Hanna Hoot, why can't you leave Jake alone?" Carlos asked angrily. "He's got enough to worry about. The last thing he needs is your dumb pranks."

"Where's your sense of humor, Carlos?" Hanna asked, with a toss of her red pigtails. "I was just trying to cheer him up."

"Nothing will cheer me up," Jake said, "until I can prove once and for all that Cliff Top Coasters is not haunted!"

"Why don't you stop complaining and do something about it, Jake?" Hanna asked.

Carlos groaned and rolled his eyes. And although Jake thought of Hanna as a friend, he had to admit that she could get on his nerves. Besides being bossy, Hanna loved to play practical jokes. She had an army of pranks at her fingertips, because her father owned Riverside's only joke shop, The Gag Bag. Still, she had a point.

"You're right, Hanna," Jake said. "Our parents died when I was little, and George has always been there for me. Buying the amusement park was a dream come true for him. But if people are too scared to come to Cliff Top, George will be out of business. I won't let that happen!"

"All right, Jake," Hanna said, her eyes shining. "If you don't think your brother's park is haunted, then prove it. I dare you to spend a night there and ride all the rides. Then you can tell the entire town your brother's park is not haunted—if it's not."

"I'll do it!" Jake cried. Hanna's plan was a little crazy, but if it worked, it just might help George. "Carlos, are you in?"

"Of course! What do I love better than riding roller coasters?" Carlos asked.

"Me!" Hanna said with a wink. Carlos made a face. "And I'll be there, too, to make sure you guys go through with it."

• • •

Two days later, Jake stood outside the locked gate to Cliff Top Coaters amusement park. Usually the park's gate was open, welcoming customers. The sound of music and the happy screams and laughter of children made it seem like a friendly place. But tonight was different.

Jake rubbed his hands together. The chill in the air made him shiver. He stood outside the gate of Cliff Top Coasters, waiting. In the light of day Jake didn't believe in ghosts. But as he stood there, all alone in the dark, Jake began to feel spooked.

"Ahhh!" Jake yelled, as he felt a hand grab his shoulder.

"Jake! Take it easy, man. It's just me!" Carlos said.

Jake let out a deep breath. "What took you so long? I've been waiting here for almost half an hour."

"Sorry." Carlos grinned at his friend. "Our favorite principal, Mr. Borley, gave me detention again! He made me help paint the gymnasium."

Jake smiled. He hoped never to have one of Mr. Borley's famous punishments.

"I don't know if I trust Hanna, Jake," Carlos said. "This entire dare might be one of her practical jokes."

"Hanna is my friend and she knows how worried I am about George," Jake said. "She might try to pull a few gags on us, but when it comes down to it, I think we can trust her."

• • • • • • • • • •

"I wouldn't be too sure about that!" Carlos said. "I don't want her pranks getting in our way."

Just then, the boys heard a rustling noise coming from the trees next to the park entrance. They looked at each other as the noise grew louder and louder.

"Is someone there?" Jake called out. There was no answer.

Jake and Carlos heard twigs snapping and leaves rustling. Suddenly, a snarling wolf charged out of the trees. The boys screamed and grabbed on to each other.

"Ha, ha, ha," the wolf cried, laughing.

Jake got an angry look on his face. Most wolves didn't wear jeans, a sweatshirt, and sneakers. He walked over to the wolf and pulled at its face. A mask came off in his hands.

"Hi, guys," Hanna smiled. "Sorry I'm late. Ready to have some fun?"

Jake sighed. Hanna was already up to her same old tricks.

"Listen up," Hanna barked, grabbing the wolf mask from Jake and shoving it into her backpack. "I've made a map of the park, and I have copies for all of us. I've marked off our routes, so we'll be sure to hit every ride. You guys start on the north side of the park, and I'll start on the south end."

"You don't want to stick together?" Jake asked.

"No, we can cover more ground this way," Hanna replied. "Unless you guys are scared and need me to protect you."

Carlos was angry. "Now listen here, Hanna Hoot. I don't want you hanging around anywhere near us tonight."

"Calm down." Jake was used to playing the peacemaker between Carlos and Hanna. "We'll take the maps. That way if we need to find one another we can. But you'd better stay out of Mr. Finley's way, Hanna. He isn't exactly friendly, and I don't know what he'll do if he finds us in the park after hours."

Mr. Finley was the caretaker of Cliff Top Coasters. He lived in a house right next to the park. Jake and Carlos had already had a few run-ins with him over the summer.

Hanna nodded. "I'll stay out of the grump's way—don't worry."

"One more thing," Jake said. He took two keys from his pocket and handed one to Hanna.

Jake had helped himself to copies of George's master key to Cliff Top Coasters. Normally he would never take anything from his brother without asking, but Jake knew George would never agree to their plan.

"These keys can turn on any ride in the park," Jake told Hanna. "Just put it into the ride's control panel and press the green button. It will set the ride on a timer so you have time to get into it. And the timer will also stop the ride automatically."

"Then if everybody is ready, let's do this," Jake said. He walked toward the entrance and inserted the key into the lock.

The iron gates creaked as they swung open. Jake, Carlos, and Hanna stepped inside the dark, quiet park. Tonight was the night to find out if Cliff Top Coasters was really haunted, once and for all!

Are you ready to enter Cliff Top Coasters? If so, decide who you will follow through the park.

- **If you follow Jake and Carlos, go to page 9.**
- **If you follow Hanna, go to page 12.**

• • • • • • • • •

"Good luck, guys," Hanna called over her shoulder as she headed in the opposite direction. "You're going to need it!"

Carlos scowled. "Thank goodness she's gone! Now let's get started."

Jake pulled out the map Hanna had given him. He turned on his flashlight and shined it onto the map.

"She really has mapped everything out for us," said Jake. "She wants us to start at The Demonator." The Demonator, a bright-red steel coaster with orange flames painted on the cars, was famous for its intense drops.

"Who died and made Hanna Hoot boss?" Carlos muttered.

"Well, we don't have to ride The Demonator first, but we might as well start that way anyway," Jake replied.

Jake and Carlos walked through the deserted park. Usually a busy, exciting place, it now seemed desolate and eerie. Carlos shined his flashlight onto the abandoned food and souvenir stands.

"This place is a real ghost town," he said. Jake glared at him. "Sorry, bro! Wrong word—no ghosts here!"

"It's okay," Jake said. "It is more spooky here at night than I thought it would be."

• • • • • • • •

The boys stopped as they came to the Bumper Cars, located right in front of The Demonator.

"Wanna start with the Bumper Cars first before we move on to The Demonator?" Jake asked.

"Are you sure you want to?" Carlos asked with a grin. "Don't forget how I demolished you the last time we rode the Bumper Cars!"

"Oh yeah? I don't think you'll be so lucky this time," Jake retorted as he started the ride.

The boys laughed and yelled as they crashed their cars into each other over and over again. Carlos trapped Jake into a corner and then backed up his car so he could smash into Jake. At the last second, Jake managed to drive away, and Carlos crashed his car into the railing. The ride stopped, and the boys got off, laughing.

"Well, we can cross the Bumper Cars off the map," Jake said. "What's next?"

"I'd love to go on The Demonator," Carlos said. "It has to be the most terrifying coaster in the park. But no way am I taking orders from Hanna! Let's go on Monkey Business." Monkey Business was a super-fast wooden coaster that boasted some of the most awesome twists and turns of any ride in the park.

"That's my favorite coaster!" Jake smiled. "But

it does make sense to start here and work our way around by riding the rides in order. Monkey Business is in the middle of the park."

Carlos frowned. *"Hmph."*

"Well, how about The Pirate's Revenge?" Jake suggested, pointing to the swinging ship ride.

"Remember when we rode it five times in a row and you threw up?" Carlos laughed. "But seriously, Jake, tonight is about helping your brother. I'll leave the decision up to you."

How should Jake decide?

- **If Jake and Carlos ride Monkey Business, turn to page 32.**
- **If Jake and Carlos ride The Pirate's Revenge, turn to page 51.**
- **If Jake and Carlos ride The Demonator, turn to page 85.**

• • • • • • • •

"Good luck, guys!" Hanna yelled to the boys as she made her way to the south side of the park. "You're going to need it!"

Hanna laughed to herself. Alone at last! All her plans were now falling into place. She had raced over to the park after dinner and hid until the park closed for the night. After all the employees left, Hanna snuck around the park and set up some surprises for Carlos and Jake.

Now she stood alone in the dark. For a split second, Hanna felt nervous. The park seemed so unfriendly at night.

"I don't believe in ghosts!" Hanna bravely said out loud. "But after tonight, Jake and Carlos will!"

Feeling better Hanna reached around and pulled the map from her heavy backpack. Besides the wolf mask, there were a few other goodies tucked inside. She had set up as many pranks as she could, but she had called it quits before Finley made his final rounds before lights-out. She didn't want to get caught before all the fun had started.

Hanna glanced at the map in her hand. If the boys followed it, they would ride The Demonator first. She would love to see their faces when they rode that coaster. She had set up some of her best pranks on it.

• • • • • • • •

Hanna had planned to secretly follow the boys and see their reactions to her practical jokes. But Carlos was already suspicious of her. She didn't want them to catch her—yet. The Observation Tower, located in the middle of the park, would give her a great view. With her night-vision binoculars tucked into her backpack, she'd be able to see everything without the boys knowing.

Hanna looked around the deserted park. *On the other hand,* she thought, *it's not every day I'm practically all alone in an amusement park.* She could go on any ride she wanted—with no wait! And if the boys didn't stick to the map and caught up with her, it would look like she was keeping her end of the deal.

Practical joker Hanna has a decision to make. What do you think Hanna should do?

- **If Hanna follows Jake and Carlos, turn to page 45.**
- **If Hanna decides to watch the boys from the Observation Tower, turn to page 26.**
- **If Hanna decides to ride some rides, turn to page 23.**

"She could be in serious trouble, Carlos," Jake said, running in the direction of the screams. "And we've got to help her!"

Carlos shook his head and ran after his friend. They found Hanna standing in front of the Haunted House.

"It was a ghost—a real ghost!" Hanna shrieked, her face pale. "It walked out of the Haunted House and went behind The Pirate's Revenge!"

Carlos sneered. "Please, Hanna. You think we're going to fall for another one of your pranks?"

Hanna shook her head. "I swear this isn't one of my pranks. You've got to believe me."

Jake and Carlos looked at each other. They had never seen Hanna so scared.

"Well, you did see a strange light there, Carlos," Jake said. "Maybe we should go back to The Pirate's Revenge and have a look around."

"Okay, let's check it out," Carlos said. Then he turned to Hanna. "But I'm warning you, Hanna Hoot, if this is one of your pranks . . . "

"I wish it was," Hanna said with a shudder.

Quietly, they walked back along the path to The Pirate's Revenge. Behind the ride, they saw a strange glowing figure moving toward the fence that separated the park from the woods. It walked right through the fence and into the woods beyond!

Jake, Carlos, and Hanna gasped and huddled together. "Could that be a *real* ghost?" Jake whispered

"I don't know anything else that can walk through fences," Carlos said.

"This is too creepy," Hanna said. "I never thought there would be real ghosts here. I was just hoping to scare you guys silly."

"Ha! I knew it!" Carlos said triumphantly. "Jake, how many times did I tell you—"

"Stop!" Jake cried. "We need to follow the ghost!"

Unlike the ghost, Jake, Carlos, and Hanna had to climb over the fence. The woods were dark and spooky. Soon they saw the glowing light again and followed it. The ghostly figure had stopped. The kids hid behind a tree to sneak a look at the phantom.

The glowing figure was a man wearing old-fashioned pants that were short and tattered at the ends. His shirt was white with puffy sleeves, and he wore a bandana tied around his head. He looked like an old-time sailor.

"My bones, my bones, oh where are my bones?" He moaned. He picked a shovel up from the ground and began digging.

Hanna started to shake. At first, Jake thought she was trembling with fear, but Hanna pointed to her nose. Then she let out a loud sneeze!

The ghost looked toward the tree and slowly began walking toward them.

"Let's get out of here," Carlos whispered urgently.

Jake shook his head. "No way. Ghost or not, I want to talk to him and find out what he's doing here!"

Should the kids face the ghost or run for their lives?

- **If Jake tries to talk to the ghost, turn to page 69.**
- **If Jake, Carlos, and Hanna run away, turn to page 103.**

• • • • • • • • •

Jake had a funny feeling he just couldn't shake—that Carlos had disappeared while he was riding Monkey Business. The only way to find out for sure was for Jake to ride the coaster.

Inserting the key into the control panel, Jake started the coaster. Shaking with fear, he climbed into a car. The ride took off. Jake felt his panic rise as the coaster turned and plunged him into complete darkness. *Carlos might have vanished in this very spot,* Jake thought. Thankfully, the coaster emerged from the dark pit after a few seconds.

Jake forced himself to keep his eyes open and look around for any clues, but what he really felt like doing was closing his eyes and screaming his head off in terror. After what seemed like hours, the cars finally returned to the entrance. Jake breathed a sigh of relief. Even though he didn't find Carlos, at least he hadn't disappeared, too!

Jake climbed out of the car. Carlos was standing right there!

"Carlos?" Jake asked. "I thought something had happened to you. Where were you?"

Carlos did not look happy. "George stopped Monkey Business and made me get off," he muttered.

Jake's eyes widened. "George?" he asked in disbelief.

• • • • • • • •

"That's right, Jake," Jake's brother George stepped out from the shadows behind Carlos. A group of kids were standing next to him.

Jake gulped. George looked furious.

"After I caught Carlos here, we left to look for you," George said. "Then we heard the coaster and came back to wait."

"But what are these kids doing here?" Jake recognized some of them from school. He glanced over at the boys and girls. Most of them were red-faced and looking at the ground. And standing in the middle of the group was Derek!

"We were just having fun," he said defiantly.

"Until your brother caught us," one teary-eyed girl added. "Oh, I knew we were going to get in trouble!" she wailed and burst into tears.

"I've been coming to the park the past few nights to find out what's been going on," George explained. "Tonight I finally caught these kids—they've been sneaking into the park at night to ride for free."

"So *that's* why people have been saying the park is haunted," Jake said. "They've been turning on the rides and screaming. Derek told everyone in school that the park was haunted, when he was behind it the entire time! He almost put you out of business, George!"

• • • • • • • • • •

"Don't worry, I've already called the police," George said. "They'll deal with Derek. But you and Carlos are in trouble, too. Carlos has already explained why you came here tonight, Jake. I understand you thought you were helping me. But coming here alone at night was a risky thing to do. You should have known better."

"I'm sorry, George," Jake said.

"And I hear that Hanna Hoot is in the park tonight, too," George said. Jake nodded. "We'll go and find her right now. She can share in your punishment."

Jake and Carlos glanced at each other in alarm. Whatever George had planned, it wouldn't be good!

"At first I was going to ban you all from the park for an entire year," George said. Carlos groaned. "But I've come up with a better idea."

"What?" Jake asked warily.

"We've had a lot of people throwing up on the more intense coasters," George said. "I'm going to give you, Carlos, and Hanna buckets and mops—and put you on puke patrol!"

THE END

• • • • • • • •

Nothing was going to spoil her good time, Hanna decided as she walked out of the Hedge Maze. She was having too much fun—and she wasn't about to leave now.

Walking toward the center of the park, Hanna spied the carnival games. Brightly colored booths held games of chance. Hanna ran over to them.

Hanna chose a booth that had funny clowns on it. On the top of each clown head was a deflated balloon. To win the game, you had to shoot water from a water gun into the clown's mouth. This filled up the balloon. The first person to fill up their balloon all the way was the winner.

Hanna picked up a squirt gun and aimed it at the clown's mouth. She pulled the trigger to shoot water at the clown, but nothing happened.

"Dumb game," Hanna complained, banging the gun against the table. "Nothing is going right for me tonight."

Hanna dropped the water gun and began to walk away, but a rustling noise made her stop and spin around. Floating in midair was the water gun! A spray of cold water hit her in the face.

Hanna wiped water from her face and screamed, running away from the clown game. *This is more than some dumb prank,* she thought in terror. *Cliff Top Coasters really* is *haunted!*

• • • • • • • • •

Suddenly Hanna felt something whiz by her face. She turned around. She was standing in front of the dart game. Sharp darts were shooting past her head! Hanna screamed and ran past another booth. This time, basketballs bounded at her from the Hoop Shot game.

"Help! Jake, Carlos, help me please!" Hanna sobbed, blocking the balls with her arms.

Carlos and Jake were just about to get on The Labyrinth, a steel loop-de-loop coaster, when they heard Hanna's screams.

"Can you believe she's trying to trick us again?" Carlos snorted. "Does she really think we're that stupid?"

Still screaming for help, Hanna began to panic. She ran in circles and found herself back at the water-gun game. A low rumbling filled the air. The clowns from the game began to free themselves from their posts. They had come to life!

Hanna backed up in terror as the clowns, with white faces, big red noses, and evil grins, rushed at her. Hanna turned to run, but discovered she'd backed herself against a cotton-candy stand in the corner.

The clowns crowded around her. Hanna screamed, as their pale white faces came closer . . .

• • •

• • • • • • • • •

Later that night, Jake and Carlos were being questioned by the Riverside Police. When the boys couldn't find Hanna, they'd called George, who had called Hanna's parents. She was not at home. The police were called, and they were searching the park.

"We've found the girl!" a police officer cried.

Jake, Carlos, and George rushed after the other police officers. A huge mound of fluffy pink cotton candy was lumped on the floor. The officers pulled a pale-looking Hanna out of the sticky pile.

"The clowns came to life! They trapped me in this cotton candy!" she babbled. "I've been here for hours. I want to go home!"

Sitting on the ground was a clown nose.

Once Hanna's story got out, nobody wanted to come to Cliff Top Coasters, day or night. George had to close the business, and he and Jake left town.

THE END

• • • • • • • •

"How many times will I get a chance like this?" Hanna asked out loud. She could ride all her favorite rides and still have the rest of the night to watch Jake and Carlos get fooled by her jokes!

There was only one problem: deciding which ride to go on first. The park was packed with terrific rides. Her all-time favorite ride was the Merry-Go-Round, but now that she was older, she'd been too embarrassed to ride it. Tonight she could ride it all night long, and no one would know! Splash Down, the log flume, was Hanna's second favorite ride, and usually she had to wait on a very long line. No wait tonight! Or she could ride The Demonator just to show Jake and Carlos that she wasn't afraid.

Help Hanna have a little fun before her night of pranks begins! Choose which ride she should go on.

- **If Hanna takes a spin on the Merry-Go-Round, turn to page 40.**
- **If Hanna rides Splash Down, turn to page 81.**
- **If Hanna decides to brave The Demonator, turn to page 73.**

• • • • • • • • •

A joke's a joke, but Hanna knew it wouldn't be funny if Mr. Finley caught Jake and Carlos in the park after hours. Ducking down to avoid Mr. Finley, Hanna caught up to Jake and Carlos. She hid behind a tree and called out to them.

"Guys—*pssssst*! It's me, Hanna," she whispered loudly.

Jake stopped and looked over at Hanna. "What are you doing here?"

"Quiet!" Hanna said. "Mr. Finley just came out of that shed over there. You've got to hide."

Jake and Carlos ran behind the tree just in time. They all ducked as Mr. Finley walked by. He was carrying a large object, and he walked behind the shed with it. He came back out, his arms empty, and went back into the shed.

"What can he be up to at this time of night?" Carlos whispered. "Let's see what he put back there."

The three kids sneaked next to The Demonator and hid behind a section of coaster track right next to the shed. Mr. Finley appeared again, this time holding a large stereo. He placed it on the ground next to two stereo speakers.

Suddenly Hanna got really excited. "It's Finley!" Hanna hissed at the boys. "He's been haunting Cliff Top Coasters!"

• • • • • • • •

"How'd you figure that out, Sherlock?" Carlos whispered back.

"I can tell when someone is planning a prank," Hanna replied, "and believe me, he's up to no good. Let's go stop him!"

"Not so fast," Jake said. "Let's wait and watch. I want to see what he's going to do."

Do you think Mr. Finley is haunting the park? Choose a page and find out if you're right!

- **If Jake, Carlos, and Hanna confront Mr. Finley, turn to page 114.**
- **If Jake, Carlos, and Hanna watch and wait, turn to page 90.**

• • • • • • • •

Hanna tucked the map into her backpack and began to walk toward the Observation Tower. She didn't want to miss a minute of Jake and Carlos being scared out of their minds—especially Carlos. He had no sense of humor at all.

The Observation Tower was located in the center of the park. Guests could ride to the top and get a view of the entire park and even of the river and the town below.

Hanna rode to the top and took her night-vision binoculars out of her backpack. She trained them to the north side of the park but could not see the boys.

They must not be following my instructions, Hanna thought with a frown.

She swung around and continued to look through the binoculars. The boys were walking along the east side of the park, heading toward the southeast end where the log flume and the Hedge Maze were located.

Hanna let out a whoop of delight. The Hedge Maze! She had planted some awesome tricks there, including a fog machine and some motion-activated pranks. Although Hanna could see pretty well from the tower with her binoculars, she couldn't resist getting a closer look. She rode the tower's elevator back down to the bottom.

Hanna ran out of the Observation Tower and headed toward the Hedge Maze. The perfectly trimmed hedges, dotted with red berries, were grown into a tricky maze. There was no sign of the boys. Hiding behind a bush, Hanna waited.

After ten minutes, Hanna began to get restless—and a little scared. The Hedge Maze was in a remote corner of the park, and it was pitch black since Hanna had shut off her flashlight so Jake and Carlos wouldn't be able to spot her. Usually Hanna laughed at the thought of ghosts, but now she began to grow uneasy. Anything could sneak up on her in the dark.

Where were Jake and Carlos? Maybe the boys weren't coming to the maze after all. All her hard work would be wasted. Worse, she didn't want to wait much longer in the dark.

Then Hanna got an idea. She could enter the hedge maze and cry for help. Jake would definitely come running to help her, and Carlos would probably follow him. It was a good plan, but Hanna felt a twinge of guilt about tricking Jake that way. He really was worried about his brother.

• • • • • • • •

Maybe I should just keep waiting, she thought. Jake and Carlos were bound to come to the Hedge Maze soon. And she could use her night-vision binoculars to see in the dark.

- **If Hanna screams for help to lure Jake and Carlos to the Hedge Maze, turn to page 78.**
- **If she keeps waiting for them to show up, turn to page 54.**

• • • • • • • • •

Hanna rushed past Jake and Carlos. She didn't stop to fill them in on her adventures until they were all safely outside and away from the Haunted House.

"Usually, I'd never believe a story like that from you, Hanna," said Carlos. "But we've had some unbelievable things happen to us, too."

Jake went on to explain how while the boys were riding the mini-coaster, Bugging Out, the cute little ladybug car they were in began to buzz like a real bug. It flew through the air and landed at the doorstep of the Haunted House.

"We'd better get out of here before whatever locked Hanna in comes back," Jake said, glancing around.

The kids left the park and went straight to Jake's house to tell George. George, grumpy from being woken up, would not believe the kids at first. But Jake was persistent, and George finally agreed to look into it, if only to assure his little brother.

The very next night, George spent the next night at Cliff Top with a team of ghostbusters. The ghostbusters said the park was indeed haunted and performed an exorcism. George was still skeptical, but after that night, weeks went by and nothing unusual happened at the park. People began to

• • • • • • • • •

Hanna slowly climbed down the creaky stairway leading into the Haunted House's basement. When she reached the bottom, she shined her flashlight beam around the dusty cellar. Cobwebs littered every corner, and boxes were stacked up against the walls. *They must use this as a storage room*, Hanna thought.

SLAM! Another loud noise jolted Hanna. This time it was accompanied by a cackling laugh.

Shining her flashlight up the staircase, Hanna could see that the door was now shut. She ran up the stairs and tried to open it, but of course it was locked.

"Not again!" Hanna cried. She banged and pounded on the door. There was no response. Finally, Hanna went back down the basement stairs. She looked around for a cellar door that would lead outside. There was nothing—not even a window.

Hanna hiked back up the stairs and pounded on the door again, yelling for help. After what seemed like hours, the door finally opened. It was Carlos and Jake!

"Hanna, are you okay?" Jake asked.

"What do you think?" Hanna snapped. "Jake, you better tell your brother George something very strange is happening at Cliff Top Coasters!"

• • •

come back to Cliff Top Coasters and soon business was better than ever.

When it seemed the park was free from ghosts once and for all, Jake and Carlos were finally able to convince Hanna to visit the park again.

"Well, Hanna," Jake said, as they waited in line to ride The Pirate's Revenge. "Should we try the Haunted House next?"

"Absolutely," Hanna said with a smile. "But this time, I'll stay out of the basement!"

THE END

• • • • • • • • • •

"Well, Monkey Business is my favorite coaster," Jake said. "We can go to The Demonator when we're done."

The boys ran to Monkey Business. A wooden monkey hung by its tail over the entrance. Yellow bananas and funny monkeys decorated the cars. The wooden track curved out of view, but Jake knew from experience that the ride contained twists, turns, and great drops.

After Jake started the ride, he and Carlos got into the first car and held on tightly. Monkey Business was a bumpy ride.

When the ride ended, Carlos turned to Jake. "Let's go again!"

Jake agreed. After all, it was his favorite ride. But when the cars returned after the second time, Carlos wanted to ride yet again.

"No way," Jake said. "This is fun, but we've got work to do, remember?"

"Come on, just one more time!" Carlos pleaded.

Jake sighed. "Fine, ride one more time," he said. "But you can go by yourself. I'm going to look around while you're on the ride."

While Carlos took off on the coaster, Jake walked around. Carnival games surrounded the ride, ranging from darts and hoops to games of

• • • • • • • • •

chance. Jake walked through the area, shining his flashlight onto the empty booths.

Suddenly Jake realized that he had wandered pretty far from Monkey Business. Although he could still hear the zooming cars, he started to grow a little uneasy about being in the dark all alone.

Out of the corner of his eye, Jake thought he saw something move. Startled he swung his flashlight around. But nothing was there.

Spooked, it now seemed to Jake that the dark shadows of the park loomed up at him. A cool breeze blew over him and he shivered. *Maybe ghosts do exist*, he thought. He shook his head and told himself to stop thinking crazy thoughts. *It's just the eerie atmosphere getting to you*, he told himself. Still, he'd feel a lot better searching the park with Carlos by his side. He walked back to the coaster to get his friend.

As he approached the ride, he saw that the coaster cars were back at the starting point. But Carlos wasn't there.

"Carlos?" Jake called. He shined his flashlight into the cars and up and down the platform. Carlos was gone!

Jake trembled. He took a deep breath to calm himself. *Carlos must have gotten off the coaster*

• • • • • • • • •

when the cars returned to the platform, Jake reasoned to himself.

But as hard as he tried, Jake couldn't block out another terrifying possibility. What if Carlos has just vanished—*while* he was riding the coaster?

I could ride the coaster myself to find out what happened, Jake thought. *But what if I disappear, too?*

What should Jake do?

- **If Jake rides Monkey Business again, turn to page 17.**
- **If Jake searches for Carlos on foot, turn to page 96.**

"The entire point of being here tonight is to find out if the park is haunted or not. This strange light is our first clue," Carlos argued. "Listen, Hanna has stopped screaming. I told you it was just another one of her pranks!"

"I guess you're right," Jake said. "I'm here to help my brother. And Hanna has already proven why she's here—to play tricks on us!"

Jake and Carlos slowly began to search the grass around The Pirate's Revenge. Jake heard footsteps. He grabbed Carlos's arm and pointed to the front of the ride.

A tall, hooded figure walked by, carrying a flashlight. Carlos nodded at Jake, and the two of them silently followed the figure to The Demonator. Jake and Carlos ducked behind a bush to watch what would happen next.

The hooded person started the coaster. The flaming cars went roaring off into the night sky. Then the stranger pulled out a boom box and turned it on. Scary screams filled the air. Carlos and Jake looked at each other in amazement. They'd found the "ghost"—but who was it?

Jake and Carlos gasped as the figure reached up and removed its hood. It was Mr. Borley, their middle school principal!

. . . .

"This should put Cliff Top Coasters out of business for good," Mr. Borley muttered, as he fiddled with the dials on the boom box. "I can buy the park for cheap—and turn it into a new football field for the school. And to top it off, no more students will be cutting class to come to this park! This is one of the best ideas I've ever had."

Jake could not believe it. Mr. Borley was the ghost! But how could they stop him?

"Let's find Mr. Finley. He'll know what to do," Jake whispered to Carlos.

"Forget him! You know how he is—he'll just yell at us for being in the park after hours," Carlos whispered back. "We should go find Hanna. She has a cell phone, and we can call your brother."

Who should Jake and Carlos go to for help?

- **If Jake and Carlos go get Mr. Finley for help, turn to page 75.**
- **If they go find Hanna instead, turn to page 116.**

• • • • • • • • •

"I came here tonight to help my brother," Jake said. "Let's open the door."

"I'll help," Carlos said. He struggled to stand and then sat back, groaning.

"You'd better not move," Hanna said to Carlos. She handed him her cell phone. "Keep trying to call for help. We'll be right back."

Jake opened the door and climbed down a set of crude-looking stairs. Hanna followed him. They found themselves in a small room that had been dug into the ground. There was something in the middle of the dirt floor, half buried in the ground. It looked like a huge bone!

A man was bent over the bone. Hearing the kids, he stood up. Jake gasped. It was Mr. Snoggle, the former owner of Cliff Top Coasters!

"So you've found my little secret, huh?" the man asked with a mean smile.

"I don't know what your secret is, but my friend is hurt. You're going to be in big trouble!" Jake said.

"You friend is small potatoes compared to what I've found," Mr. Snoggle said. "Do you know what this is?" He pointed at the bone in the floor.

"A bone?" Jake asked.

"Not any old bone, but the bone of a Tyrannosaurus rex," Mr. Snoggle replied. "In fact, I believe the complete skeleton is buried under here. Do you know how much private collectors would pay for a T-rex skeleton? Millions!" Mr. Snoggle chuckled happily.

"This is my brother's park now, Mr. Snoggle. The bones don't belong to you," Jake said angrily.

"That's why I had to create a little haunting. And when everyone in Riverside is too scared to come to the park, George will be begging me to buy this place back from him!" Mr. Snoggle said nastily.

"Why did you sell the park to George in the first place?" Hanna asked.

"I didn't find the first bone until right after I had sold the park to George. But I came up with a plan—only now you kids could spoil it all. I can't let that happen," Mr. Snoggle said. "I'm going to lock you two down here, along with your friend, until I can figure out what to do with you." He walked toward them menacingly.

A loud noise from above stopped Mr. Snoggle in his tracks.

"Stop right there!" George Jagger yelled. He ran down the stairs into the small room. "You're the one who's going to be locked up."

Suddenly, police officers swarmed into the room. An officer slapped handcuffs on Mr. Snoggle. He

• • • • • • • • •

turned and glared at Jake and Hanna as the policeman hustled him up the stairs.

George led Jake and Hanna out of the small room. Carlos was still sitting there, but someone had draped a blanket around his shoulders.

"It turns out we didn't need the cell phone," Carlos said. "Our parents found out we were missing and called the police."

"The Vegas and the Hoots were worried sick!" George said. "Mrs. Hoot insisted on calling the police. But luckily Mr. Hoot found a copy of the map to the park in Hanna's bedroom. That's when they called me. So we came here to look for you."

Just then a police officer walked up to the group. She took their statements about the night's events. Then they were free to go home.

"So what are you going to do about the dinosaur bones, George?" Jake asked as they left the park.

"I'll have some scientists come and examine the bone. If it is a dinosaur bone, we'll donate it to a museum," George said.

"Why not build a museum here?" Jake asked.

Hanna laughed. "Yeah, George, it will make your park even more *dino*mite!"

THE END

• • • • • • • • •

Hanna couldn't resist riding the Merry-Go-Round. She ran back toward the park entrance.

Visitors saw the Merry-Go-Round as soon as they walked into Cliff Top Coasters. The beautiful horses and the cheerful music welcomed people into the park.

Before she started the ride, Hanna looked around to make sure Carlos and Jake were gone. She didn't want them to see her riding a baby ride! Then she climbed onto the back of her favorite horse, a brown one with flowers in its mane. The merry music played, and the ride slowly spun around. Hanna's horse began to bob up and down. Hanna grinned. This was a great idea!

Suddenly the music, which began as a happy tune, changed to a more ominous melody. Then Hanna's horse and the other horses on the ride began to light up as if an inner light inside of them had suddenly turned on.

What's happening? Hanna thought. She tightly gripped the reins of her horse. Suddenly her horse began to snort and toss its head. The horse was alive!

Hanna hung on for dear life as the horse jumped off, freeing itself from the carousel. It galloped madly through the park. Screaming, Hanna shut her eyes tightly and clutched the horse to keep from falling. The horse finally slowed down, and Hanna found the courage to open her eyes. The horse was heading toward the Haunted House!

The horse picked up speed again and ran around to the back of the house. It sailed over the broken-down fence surrounding the backyard and stopped. Hanna quickly dismounted. The horse snorted and tossed its head one last time. Then it completely vanished!

Hanna rubbed her eyes. Was she seeing things? No—Hanna's heart was pounding, and she knew that however strange the events of the last few minutes were, they were real. But why did the horse bring her here? Hanna glanced around at the backyard of the Haunted House. It was a fake graveyard with ancient-looking tombstones scattered about. A few skeletal hands were sticking out of the dirt. Even though she knew the graveyard and its props were fake, Hanna shivered.

Suddenly an eerie whisper came from deep within the graveyard. *"Haaaannnnaaa Hooooot,"* a low voice whispered eerily. *"Haannnaaa Hooooot."*

Goosebumps broke out all over Hanna's arms. Someone was calling her name!

Hanna looked around wildly. Who was calling

her? The back door to the Haunted House was wide open, and a dim light was glowing inside. Hanna thought of running into the house to escape the creepy voice. But who—or what—was calling her name?

Should Hanna follow the whispers in the graveyard? Or should she escape into the Haunted House instead?

- **If Hanna goes into the Haunted House, turn to page 60.**
- **If Hanna follows the whispers and goes deeper into the graveyard, turn to page 94.**

• • • • • • • • •

"We can't go off with a crazy stranger in the middle of the night!" Jake told Carlos. "What are you thinking?"

"You're right," Carlos said. "Let's call the police."

Dr. Jasper gave a cry of alarm. He quickly turned and gave Carlos a hard kick on the shin. Carlos fell and grabbed his leg.

"Ouch!" he cried.

Dr. Jasper took off running. Jake chased after him, but as before, the scientist managed to disappear into the shadows of the park. Panting, he ran back to Carlos.

"We'd better get help," Jake said. He helped Carlos to his feet. The two boys made their way to the house of the park's caretaker, Mr. Finley's.

Soon Cliff Top Coasters was swarming with police. At first no one believed Jake and Carlos's story. But George examined some of his coasters and did indeed find some strange devices attached to them.

"That Dr. Jasper was definitely up to something weird at Cliff Top Coasters," George said.

The police caught Dr. Jasper at his laboratory. They had to drag him away, screaming.

The story was big news in Riverside for days.

Thanks to the eccentric scientist and his wacky experiments, people crowded Cliff Top Coasters. Business was better than ever!

THE END

• • • • • • • •

"I've just got to see Carlos and Jake's reaction to my gags," Hanna said to herself gleefully. She didn't want to miss seeing the two of them scared out of their mind, and watching from the Observation Tower just wouldn't cut it. She wanted to be up close and personal!

Hanna sneaked back to the north side of the park, staying in the shadows. She could hear the boys talking.

"Jake, throw out that dumb map," Carlos said. "I'm not taking orders from Hanna."

"We could go on Flight of the Fairies first," Jake suggested.

Hanna trailed the boys as they walked to the stand-up steel roller coaster. Purple and pink swinging cars were suspended from a tubular track.

Rats! Hanna thought. Flight of the Fairies was one of the rides she didn't have time to prank. The boys climbed in, and the over-the-shoulder restraints locked. With a *whoosh*, the boys flew off. Hanna fumbled around in her backpack and pulled out a stink bomb.

Hanna frowned. She wanted all her pranks tonight to be spooky. She shrugged. *Oh, well.* With a smile, she placed the stink bomb on the ground. Then, holding her nose, she smashed it with her foot. She ran behind a bench to hide and watch the fun.

When the ride ended, Jake and Carlos walked off, holding their noses. The horrible odor from Hanna's stink bomb filled the air. Carlos started to cough and make faces, and Hanna had to cover her mouth so they couldn't hear her laughing.

"What's that smell?" Jake said, gasping.

"I don't know, but let's get out of here!" Carlos said in a choked voice.

The boys began to run down the path. Hanna, laughing quietly to herself, emerged from her hiding spot, and stealthily followed the coughing and sputtering pair. The boys didn't stop until they'd reached The Demonator clear across the park. Hanna ducked behind a bench.

Suddenly Hanna saw something moving out of the corner of her eye. A door to a maintenance shed opened next to The Demonator. A man stepped out. It was Mr. Finley!

Hanna's eyes flew toward the boys. They hadn't seen Mr. Finley, but he hadn't seen them, either—yet. Hanna stayed hidden behind the bench. If she moved quickly, she could warn Jake and Carlos. But is she did that, they'd know she was spying on them.

And they'd probably figure out that she had set the stink bomb, too. Should she save her friends—or herself?

Should Hanna warn Jake and Carlos that Mr. Finley is nearby?

- **If Hanna warns the boys, turn to page 24.**
- **If Hanna does not warn Jake and Carlos, turn to page 109.**

• • • • • • • • •

"I'm sorry, Arnie," Jake said. "But what you did was wrong—and you almost put my brother out of business."

"Aha!" Hanna called triumphantly. "I've finally got a signal on my cell phone." She began to dial.

Arnie looked around, panicked. "I'm sorry about your brother—but I can't go to jail!" He took off running.

Jake was about to chase after him, but then he decided to let the police handle it. At least he had proven that Cliff Top Coasters was not haunted!

When George Jagger and the police did arrive, there was no sign of Arnie. In the underground room they found recordings of eerie screams and the lighting system that Arnie had used to "haunt" the park.

"Thank you, guys," George said to Jake, Carlos, and Hanna. "But you never should have done this by yourselves. Carlos got hurt, and you're lucky nothing worse happened."

"I'm okay, George," Carlos said. "A little bump on the head was worth it to keep Cliff Top Coasters open!"

THE END

Hanna got up from her hiding spot and approached Jake and Carlos. Their backs were to her, so she tapped Carlos's shoulder. He screamed and jumped into the air.

"Relax, Carlos, it's just Hanna," Jake said.

"Hanna! I should have known. Those ghouls we saw on The Demonator were pranks of yours, weren't they?" Carlos asked angrily.

"Yes, they were, but not all of them," Hanna said nervously.

Hanna explained, but Jake and Carlos just glared at her.

"Yeah, right," Carlos said. "This is probably part two of your master joke plan."

"I think you should leave, Hanna," Jake added.

Hanna opened her mouth to protest, but she never got the chance. All of a sudden, the sky was filled with white, screeching creatures. They looked just like the ghostly figure Hanna had seen floating next to The Demonator!

Hanna and the boys screamed and ducked, waving their arms in the air to ward off the creatures.

Hanna's hand brushed one of the ghostly creatures, and she looked up cautiously. That's when she realized the ghosts weren't ghosts at all.

• • • • • • • • • •

They were bats! She called out to Jake and Carlos, and they calmed down, too, when they realized what the creatures really were.

A month later, business at Cliff Top Coasters was booming. Hanna, Jake, and Carlos had told George about the unusual bats. When George had the bats investigated, it was discovered that the woods next to the park were home to a very rare albino bat colony.

The lights people thought they saw were really the white bats flying, and the screams they heard were the bats' cries. George installed viewing decks, and people and scientists came from all around the world—to see the bats and to have fun at Cliff Top Coasters!

THE END

• • • • • • • • •

"Let's try The Pirate's Revenge," Jake said. "I'm not going to throw up this time. I promise."

"You'd better not," Carlos said. "And if you do, aim it away from me, please. I really don't want to get puked on."

The boys walked to the ride. Suddenly they were plunged into darkness. Jake's flashlight had died!

In the dark, Jake lost his footing. He stumbled off the path. All of a sudden, he felt two long scratchy hands reaching for him. Yelling, he tried to fight them off.

"Jake! Relax!" Carlos turned his flashlight on. "It's just a bush."

Jake looked around. He had walked right into some shrubs next to the path.

"Sorry, Carlos," Jake said sheepishly. "This place is a little scary in the dark."

They reached The Pirate's Revenge. Jake started the ride, and they climbed in. A sea serpent's head was carved into the wood on each end of the swinging ship. A flag decorated with a skull and crossbones hung from the top of the ship.

The ride slowly started swinging back and forth. Jake and Carlos screamed as it began to swing higher and higher. Finally, it swung up to its maximum height. As the ship dropped, a glowing skeleton popped up in the seat in front of them!

• • • • • • • • •

Jake and Carlos screamed again, this time in terror. Flailing his arms around wildly, Jake accidentally brushed against the skeleton. He stopped screaming. It was plastic!

"It's a fake, Carlos!" Jake yelled, as the ship continued to swing. "Plastic!"

"Two words; Hanna Hoot! She must have rigged it to go off when the ship took the first big drop. Just wait until I get my hands on her," Carlos said threateningly.

"Hey—what was that?" Jake asked, looking down below. "I saw a flash of light coming from underneath the ship!"

"I see it too," Carlos said excitedly. "We'd better check it out."

When the ride finally stopped, Jake and Carlos hauled the plastic skeleton off the swinging ship and started walking toward where they'd seen the light.

Just then, piercing screams calling for help filled the air.

"That sounds like Hanna!" Jake exclaimed.

"Yeah, I'd recognize her big mouth anywhere," Carlos said. "Forget it, Jake. It's another one of her pranks."

"Maybe, but we should make sure she's all right," Jake said, as the screams continued.

. . . .

"I'm not going to let her keep making a fool of me," Carlos said stubbornly. "I say we should investigate the light. It could answer the mystery of Cliff Top Coasters!"

Who is right—Carlos or Jake? Make your choice carefully.

- **If Jake and Carlos try to help Hanna, turn to page 14.**
- **If they investigate the light, turn to page 35.**

• • • • • • • • •

Hanna decided she could wait a little longer. Besides, it just wasn't cool to pretend to call for help like a big wimp.

Just as Hanna was about to give up, she heard footsteps entering the Hedge Maze. Jake and Carlos were falling into her trap at last! With a giggle, she crouched down and waited for the fun to start. But after awhile her smile turned into a frown. She could hear her gags going off, but she didn't hear the boys screaming in fear. She stood up and looked around, and had to hold back a scream herself.

Three glowing, ghostly figures floated through the Hedge Maze, three feet off the ground! Hanna looked for wires or any other sign that these ghosts were a joke, but she didn't see a thing.

"Hanna Hoot," one moaned, pointing at her. "You are disturbing us with your mean pranks."

"H-How do I know this isn't some trick?" Hanna stammered.

The ghost reached out to touch her, and its hand went right through her! Hanna shivered.

"Go now," another ghost said. "Leave us in peace."

"O-Okay." Hanna stood. The sooner she got out of there, the better. But then the thought of Jake and his brother flashed through her mind, and she summoned up all of her courage.

"I'll leave, but only if you answer my questions," she said to the spirits. "What are you doing here, and why do you want me to leave?"

"We were on vacation for a few weeks," said a ghost. "And we came to Cliff Top Coasters. This park is wonderful!"

"Yes!" another ghost chimed in. "Cliff Top Coasters has been so much fun! Until tonight."

"We've had the park to ourselves until you kids came along," the first ghost said. "You make too much noise! And your pranks are ruining the rides!"

"A pie hit me in the face as I rode on the Merry-Go-Round!" a ghost complained. "Or it would have, if I wasn't a ghost."

Hanna looked nervous. The pie was meant for Jake and Carlos, not some ghost! "*Uhhh*, sorry about that," she stammered. "But you are going to put Cliff Top Coasters out of business. Because of you, people are saying the park is haunted, and they won't come here, even in the daytime!"

The ghosts huddled together and talked in whispers.

"We are very sorry," one of the ghosts finally replied. "We did not know we were causing any trouble. We will leave tonight."

"But we'll be watching you, Hanna Hoot," the

first ghost said. "Jokes are funny, but not when they hurt people. Be careful."

With that, all three ghosts floated out of the Hedge Maze and into the dark sky.

Ghosts—on vacation? Hanna couldn't believe it. And no one else would, either.

And no pranks! That was worse than a million ghosts.

Hanna met up with the boys later that night. She did not tell them about her experience. Weeks went by, and nothing strange happened at night again at the park. The rumors about the park went away, and business was soon booming again. Hanna didn't want to, but she gave up her practical jokes, just in case. She never knew when her ghostly friends might be watching!

THE END

• • • • • • • • • •

"Come on, Jake, look at him," Carlos whispered to his friend. "I kind of feel sorry for him; he's desperate for us to believe him. What could be the harm in looking at his 'experiments'?"

Jake glanced at Dr. Jasper, who was looking at him hopefully. The guy was pretty sad. Reluctantly, Jake agreed to go to Dr. Jasper's laboratory.

Dr. Jasper clapped his hands happily. "First, I need to get my bag. I dropped it by The Demonator. It contains the stored fear that I collected tonight."

The boys walked with the doctor back to the coaster. He picked up his bag, and then all three of them left the park.

They walked to Dr. Jasper's home. He lived nearby, right on the cliffs. His house was quiet and dark. Taking a key from his pocket, Dr. Jasper opened a side door.

"This is my laboratory," he said. He walked down a flight of stairs into a basement. The boys followed.

The room was filled with tables. The tabletops were crowded with microscopes, Bunsen burners, glass vials, and test tubes. A model of a skeleton stood in a corner. Shelves lined the walls. On the shelves were tightly sealed jars with strange objects floating inside.

• • • • • • • •

Dr. Jasper walked to a table in the middle of the room. He put his black bag on the table and opened it. Then he pulled out a mason jar from the bag. The jar was lit with a strange yellow light.

"Fear!" He placed the jar on the table and poked a few pin-sized holes into the lid. Next to the jar was a lightbulb on a stand. He connected some wires to the lightbulb and then placed the ends of the wires into the jar of fear. Muted screams filled the room, and the lightbulb began to glow.

Carlos and Jake gasped. Dr. Jasper's crazy theories were true!

"I'll be right back," Dr. Jasper said. "I've got more to show you." He walked up the stairs.

SLAM! The door shut with a bang. Jake and Carlos raced up the stairs and tried to open the door. It was locked.

A strange gas began to fill the room. Jake and Carlos coughed and put their shirts over their faces. The room started to spin, and soon both boys blacked out.

• • •

A few hours later, the sun began to rise. Jake and Carlos blinked at the bright light.

"What are you guys doing here?" Hanna asked, standing over them.

• • • • • • • • •

Jake and Carlos looked around. They were lying on the grass at the entrance of Cliff Top Coasters.

"I don't know," Jake said. "The last thing I remember is riding The Demonator."

"Me too," Carlos said.

"You must have gotten tired and took a nap," Hanna said. "I've been looking for you guys all night. The park was pretty quiet. I'd say it's definitely not haunted."

The kids made their way home. Jake and Carlos never remembered what happened to them that fateful night at Cliff Top Coasters. Strange things continued to happen at Cliff Top Coasters for a few more months, but then the mysterious events stopped. It took awhile, but business slowly returned to normal.

Soon everyone had something else to talk about. It was the opening of Jasper Power Plant. It provided energy to all of Riverside.

THE END

• • • • • • • • •

Hanna shivered and rubbed the goose bumps on her arms. No way was she following that creepy whisper! She ran up the stairs leading to the open door of the haunted house.

Hanna walked through the doorway. Straight ahead was the Haunted House kitchen. She stepped inside, then stopped. Decorated to look like an old-fashioned kitchen, there was a fireplace with a large hanging cauldron built into the wall. An animatronic witch stood by the cauldron, and Hanna knew that when the house was activated, the witch stirred the pot and cackled. But tonight, of course, she was silent.

Hanna drew a deep, steadying breath, then she took another step inside the kitchen.

BANG! Hanna jumped and spun around. The door behind her had slammed closed!

Hanna raced over to the door and tried to open it. It was locked. She banged on the door.

"Open this door! Who's there?" Hanna cried. "Somebody help!" She listened for a response to her cries, but all she heard was an unnatural silence.

Trying not to panic, Hanna looked around the room. To her right, there was a dark hallway. In the far corner, there was an open door with a staircase going down—probably to a cellar. Maybe there she'd find a door leading outside.

Something supernatural is definitely going on at the Haunted House. Help Hanna find a way out before it's too late!

- **If Hanna walks down the stairs into the cellar, turn to page 29.**
- **If Hanna goes down the hallway instead, turn to page 65.**

"Good idea," Jake told Carlos. "Let's go get that bag!"

Jake and Carlos returned to The Demonator. The black bag was in front of the coaster's control panel, right where Dr. Jasper dropped it.

Jake opened the bag. As Carlos shone his flashlight into it, Jake looked at the contents.

Jake found an envelope and handed it to Carlos. Then Jake pulled out a hammer, a wrench, and a tape recorder, along with a few other tools Jake and Carlos did not recognize.

"Open the envelope," Jake urged Carlos.

"It's a letter, addressed to Dr. Jasper," Carlos said. He read the letter out loud.

Dear Dr. Jasper,

You will get the rest of the payment when Cliff Top Coasters is officially out of business. Haunting the park was a brilliant idea. I knew it was a good idea to hire you for this job. Once Cliff Top Coasters is out of the way, my park will be the number-one amusement park again—and you will have your money. I know you need the money to fund your scientific projects, but remember—the park must be closed in order for you to collect.

• • • • • • • • •

Carlos looked at Jake. "The letter is signed 'Pamela.'"

"Pamela! That must be Pamela Pearl—the owner of Crazy Coasters!" Jake said.

"That's the park across the river!" Carlos said.

"We need to get this letter to George—fast!" Jake said. "We'd better find Hanna."

Jake and Carlos consulted the map Hanna had given them. According to her plan, Hanna would probably be riding The Labyrinth, a steel loop-de-loop coaster.

The boys ran to The Labyrinth. Luckily Hanna was there.

"What's up, guys?" she asked, climbing off the coaster.

Jake and Carlos explained about Dr. Jasper and his black bag.

"We need to leave the park right now and warn George!" Jake said.

Hanna and the boys left the park. They raced to Jake's house and woke up George. At first, George was so groggy that he didn't understand what the kids were trying to tell him. But as he became more awake, he grew alarmed.

"I'm calling the police right now!" He ran to the phone. "Do you have the letter and the bag?"

• • • • • • • • •

"Right here," Carlos said. He held up the bag. "We figure Dr. Jasper was using the tools to turn on the coasters."

"And listen to this," Jake said. He took the tape recorder out of the bag and turned it on. Ghostly screams and moans filled the air. "We think Dr. Jasper was hooking this up to the PA system in the park, so the screams could be heard in the town below."

George shook his head as he dialed the phone. Soon the police came to the house to question Jake and Carlos, and to collect the evidence. The letter alone was enough proof to arrest both Pamela Pearl and Dr. Jasper.

Jake had succeeded! He had set out to prove Cliff Top Coasters was not haunted, and he did just that! When the news got out, Cliff Top Coasters's business was booming again. With Pamela Pearl behind bars, Cliff Top Coasters's rival, Crazy Coasters, went broke and shut down.

THE END

• • • • • • • • •

Hanna wasn't taking any chances on walking down into a dark cellar—no way! She turned and walked down the hallway. It led to the Haunted House's dining room. Hanna peered into the room and was stunned by what she saw.

The room, usually a ghostly affair with cobwebs and creepy dinner entrées, was brightly lit and cheerful. A piping hot meal was on the table—and sitting around the table, ready to enjoy the feast, was a family of ghosts!

A man, woman, two children, and an elderly lady sat at the table. They wore old-fashioned clothes, kind of like the clothes the early settlers of Riverside had worn. Hanna had been to Riverside Museum on school trips and remembered the bonnets, long dresses, and breeches. Other than their odd clothes, they looked very normal—except for the fact that Hanna could see right through them!

The woman ghost turned and looked at Hanna. "I think we have company for dinner, dear," she said to the man sitting next to her.

The man stood up and offered his hand to Hanna. "Pleased to meet you. My name is Franklin Smitherson; this here is my wife, Prudence; my son, Franklin Jr.; and my daughter, Eliza. And this is my mother, Mary, but you can just call her Granny.

• • • • • • • • •

Everybody does." Hanna tried to shake the hand Mr. Smitherson offered her, but it was like trying to hold air.

"I'm Hanna Hoot," Hanna said. "W-What are you all doing here in the Haunted House?"

"You see, dear," Mrs. Smitherson said, smiling sweetly at Hanna, "this wasn't always a Haunted House. In fact, it used to be our home."

"We lived and worked here many years ago," Mr. Smitherson said. "But not in this exact spot. Our farm was over there." He pointed toward the side of the park that was now all wooded land. "One day a fire destroyed our farm. We were all in the barn when it happened and we were all killed. But our house was still standing."

"We continued living in our house," Granny piped in. "Just like when we were alive."

Mr. Smitherson nodded. "Until one day a few months ago, someone came and moved our house to this very spot."

"I remember that!" Hanna cried. "There was an article in the paper when George Jagger first began rebuilding Cliff Top Coasters. The story reported how George had moved an authentic old farmhouse from the woods to serve as the new Haunted House."

"Now all day long we have people running

around our house, dressed up like monsters!" Eliza cried.

"It's not decent," Granny added, shaking her head.

"But—the Merry-Go-Round—my horse came to life and brought me here," Hanna cried.

"Strange things have been happening since we moved here," Mr. Smitherson said. "I think it's our—what is it called, dear?"

"Ectoplasm," Mrs. Smitherson promptly replied.

"Yes, the ectoplasm. It has a strange effect on things," he said.

Hanna felt bad for the Smithersons. They seemed like nice people—or rather, nice ghosts—but she knew they couldn't stay here. She explained to them about George and how he was in danger of losing his business.

"What can we do?" Mrs. Smitherson asked sadly. "This is our home, even if they've done strange things to it. I don't want to leave."

"I have an idea," Hanna said. "Wait for me here. I'll be back soon."

Hanna ran all the way to Jake's house and woke up his brother, George.

At first George didn't believe her, but she dragged him back to the park. When they walked into the dining room of the Haunted House, the Smithersons were still there. George was shocked, but he listened to their story. Like Hanna he felt bad for them.

"I never would have moved your house if I knew you were still using it," George told the family.

George told the Smithersons he would move their house back to the woods as soon as possible. The ghostly family smiled and thanked him.

As Hanna and George left the haunted house, George thanked Hanna. "When the Smithersons and their ectoplasm are gone, Cliff Top Coasters will soon be back to normal," he said.

Standing outside were Jake and Carlos.

"G-G-George!" Jake sputtered. Carlos also looked alarmed, believing they were all in big trouble.

"Don't worry, Jake. Your punishment for sneaking into the park won't be too bad," George said. "I'm feeling pretty good right now because Hanna helped me solve the mystery at Cliff Top."

"Hanna?" Carlos was surprised.

Hanna smiled at George. "Should we tell them?"

George laughed. "We can try, but they might not believe us!"

THE END

Jake took a deep breath and stepped out from behind the tree, with Carlos and Hanna right behind him. The ghost sailor stopped in his tracks.

"My bones?" he asked the children hopefully. "Have you seen my bones?"

"I haven't seen any bones around here," Jake answered. "But who are you, and what are you doing here?"

The ghost let out a long sigh. "It's kind of a long story. My name is Samuel Watkins. I lived in Riverside many, many years ago. And when I was not much older than you, I took to the seas."

"You were a sailor?" Carlos asked.

"Aye," Samuel said. "And how I loved it! The ocean breezes, the bright sunshine! But one day I came home to visit my dear old mother. And wouldn't you know it, Farmer Thompson ran me over with his turnip cart. And I died—not in the sea but buried under a mound of turnips!"

"That's awful!" Hanna said. "But I don't understand why you're here."

"My mother buried me on the clifftop, so at least my grave could look out on the river that leads to the ocean," Samuel said sadly. "And here I stayed for many years, until someone came and disturbed my rest. Strange, loud machines dug up my bones and scattered them. Now I can't rest until they are all together again, overlooking the river."

Jake frowned. A few months ago, his brother had been adding rides to Cliff Top Coasters. It was possible that someone had disturbed Samuel's grave.

"Where was your grave?" Jake asked.

"It was under where that swinging ship now stands," Samuel said.

The Pirate's Revenge was one of the new rides added by George. They had dug up the earth there for construction. Jake had been there watching the work take place for most of the summer.

"I remember!" Jake cried. "They built The Pirate's Revenge, and then when they were done, they used dirt from the site to fill in holes left by the construction of the new Hedge Maze. Your bones are probably buried there!"

"I'll try anything," Samuel said.

The children and Samuel made their way to the Hedge Maze. On the way there, Jake asked Samuel about the strange happenings at Cliff Top Coasters.

"I do glow really brightly," Samuel explained. "And I guess I have been moaning kind of loudly at night. I'm so upset about losing my bones!"

"That still doesn't explain the coasters," Hanna piped in.

• • • • • • • •

"Those loud machines with the carts and tracks?" Samuel asked. "Sometimes when I walk by them, they turn on all by themselves."

They had reached the Hedge Maze, where they borrowed shovels from a nearby maintenance shed. Jake showed everyone the places where he remembered holes had been filled in, and everyone began to dig.

"I've found him!" Hanna cried, wiping her sweaty brow. And sure enough, there was a pile of bones in the hole she had dug. Samuel came over to inspect them.

"This is most of me," he said cheerfully, "but I'm missing a few bits."

Everyone continued to dig, and once in awhile someone would shout, "I've found a shin bone!" or "Here's a finger!" They worked well into the night, and as the sun began to come up, Jake found the last bone.

"What should we do now, Samuel?" Jake asked.

"I guess we can bury me back under the swinging ship. It's kind of fitting, me being a sailor and all," Samuel said.

They dug a hole under the ride and piled in the bones.

"I'm sorry for any trouble I caused," Samuel said.

“It’s okay,” Jake said. “I’m glad to have met you. I hope you can rest now.”

Carlos threw the last shovelful of dirt over the bones. Samuel smiled, gave a wave, and vanished completely.

Jake, Carlos, and Hanna were sweaty and dirty from their night of hard work. But they had done it! Cliff Top Coasters was now ghost-free.

“No one will ever believe us,” Jake said, “but I want George to change the name of the ride—to Samuel’s Ship!”

THE END

• • • • • • • • •

Carlos isn't the only roller-coaster daredevil around here, Hanna thought, as she made her way toward The Demonator. Even though it was dark, she could still see the ride's intense colors. Red cars with glowing orange flames painted on the sides sat on a bright red-and-orange track. As she approached the ride's entrance, she noticed Jake and Carlos walking ahead of her. Hanna ducked behind a bench and watched the boys.

This will be good, Hanna thought, as Jake and Carlos debated which ride they should go on next. Hanna would be thrilled if they chose to ride The Demonator. She had set up her best pranks on the coaster, including a holographic image that would pop up in the first car. Sitting back to watch and wait, Hanna smirked.

A strange growling noise filled the air, jolting Hanna from her thoughts. She looked around at the dark rocks and bushes surrounding the ride. Nothing. She thought about turning on her flashlight, but then the boys would spot her. She looked around again and then shrugged. It was probably nothing.

As soon as Hanna crouched behind the bench again, she heard another growl, but this time it was louder. Hanna almost laughed out loud when she

• • • • • • • •

realized what it was—her stomach! She had barely eaten any dinner that night because she was in such a hurry to get to the park and arrange her pranks.

There were some food stands on the pathway not far from the ride. Maybe she should have a little snack to tide her over. She didn't want her growling stomach to give her away!

Then again Jake and Carlos might decide to go on The Demonator, and Hanna didn't want to miss her tricks.

Should Hanna get a tasty treat or watch Jake and Carlos get tricked?

- **If Hanna watches the boys ride The Demonator, turn to page 83.**
- **If she decides to get something to eat, turn to page 88.**

• • • • • • • • •

Jake and Carlos ran to Mr. Finley's cottage. Jake knocked, and an old bearded man opened the door. He glared at the boys and barked, "What are you kids doing here?"

"Please, Mr. Finley, there's no time to explain—you've got to come with us," said Jake. "Mr. Borley, the principal of the middle school, has been haunting the park!"

Without saying a word, the caretaker slammed the door to his house and followed the boys back to The Demonator. Mr. Borley was still there.

Mr. Finley marched right over to Mr. Borley—and reached out and shook his hand!

"Good evening, sir. Can I give you a hand?" Mr. Finley asked, smiling.

"Sure. It's a great night for a haunting, Finley," Mr. Borley answered with a grin. The two men broke into laughter.

"What's going on?" Jake cried out. "I know why you're doing this, Mr. Borley, but why is Mr. Finley helping you?"

"You see, Jake," Mr. Borley began, "when I first began haunting this park, Mr. Finley did catch me. At first he was going to call the police. But I managed to talk to Mr. Finley and get him to see things my way."

• • • • • • • • • • •

"For years I've been cleaning up after disrespectful kids," Mr. Finley said. "I wouldn't mind seeing this place close down. And Mr. Borley offered me a job as custodian of the middle school if I help him out."

"You'd still have to deal with kids," Carlos pointed out.

"But at the school, Mr. Borley will give me the power to punish them. I'd love to see some of those little brats scrubbing toilets." Mr. Finley chuckled.

"Now we have a big problem," Mr. Borley said. "I guess I'll have to give you two so much homework and detention that you won't be able to find the time to tell on us."

"You're crazy if you think we're not going to tell on you," said Jake.

"Who are people going to believe—some bratty kids or the school principal?" Mr. Borley demanded.

"We'll see about that!" Jake cried. He and Carlos broke into a run.

Near the park exit, the boys crashed into Hanna. After quickly explaining to her what was going on, she used her phone to call George.

• • •

The next day, all three of them were sitting in Jake's kitchen with George.

• • • • • • • • •

"I want to be really angry at you guys for breaking into the park after hours," George said, "but you saved Cliff Top Coasters, and I'll always be grateful."

"I'm just glad you believed us," said Jake.

"Well, it's a pretty unbelievable story, but I know you'd never make something like that up for no reason," George replied. "And when the police questioned Mr. Borley and Mr. Finley, they both ratted each other out."

"What's going to happen to Mr. Borley?" Hanna asked.

"The police arrested the both of them, and I'm sure once the school board gets word of this, Mr. Borley will be looking for a new job," George said.

"I hope so," Carlos said. " I wasn't looking forward to all that homework and detention!"

Jake laughed. "You can say that again!"

THE END

• • • • • • • • •

I can't wait here all night, Hanna thought. She walked into the Hedge Maze and followed its twists and turns to the very back, being careful not to set off any of her jokes.

Then, crouching down at the end of the maze, Hanna began to scream loudly. "Help!" she cried. "Jake, Carlos, please help me!" Before long, she heard running footsteps.

"Hanna!" Jake called out. "Where are you, Hanna?"

Hanna gave another small shriek and then was quiet.

"Carlos, she's in the Hedge Maze! Follow me!" Jake yelled.

Hanna heard Jake and Carlos enter the maze. She stood up and took out her night-vision binoculars. They would never see her in the dark, but she'd sure see them!

Carlos stumbled and Hanna chuckled. He had just triggered her first prank.

Thick clouds of fog came rolling into the maze. The boys began to panic. As they zoomed around a corner to try to escape the fog, a horrible ghoul sprang out at them. It had a misshapen head and a bloody face. Its mouth was twisted in a gruesome smile to reveal a row of razor-sharp teeth. Jake and

• • • • • • • • • •

Carlos screamed and almost knocked each other over trying to get out of the creature's way. Eerie moans began to fill the air.

"Let's get out of here!" Carlos yelled in a panic.

"I'm trying," Jake answered. "But I can't find the way out!"

Hanna was laughing so hard that she had to put down her binoculars. Her pranks had worked spectacularly! Jake and Carlos were in a total panic. She sat down, clutching her stomach and laughing uncontrollably. Wiping the tears from her eyes, she finally noticed that the maze had grown quiet. She looked up to find Jake and Carlos in front of her—and they didn't look happy.

"Hanna, I really thought you needed our help." Jake looked furious.

"I knew you were up to no good tonight, Hanna!" Carlos said, even angrier than his friend.

"You know how worried I am about my brother losing the park," said Jake. "I trusted you. How could you play these jokes on me?"

"The bet is off, Hanna," Carlos said. "For you it is, anyway. We want you to leave the park immediately. Jake and I are here to find out the truth about Cliff Top Coasters—and we don't need you getting in the way."

• • • • • • • •

Hanna stood up. "Geez, guys," she mumbled. "It was just a joke. Why do you have to take things so seriously?"

"Why do you never take *anything* seriously?" Jake shot back. "Just leave the park—now."

With that, Carlos and Jake stormed out of the Hedge Maze.

Wow, they really are mad, Hanna thought, with a pang of guilt. Maybe she did go too far. But making her leave the park! That was harsh. She had every right to be here tonight. After all, the entire dare was her idea.

Should Hanna stay or go?

- **If Hanna leaves the park, turn to page 99.**
- **If Hanna decides to ignore Jake and Carlos and stay in the park, turn to page 20.**

• • • • • • • •

Hanna raced over to Splash Down. The ride's track reached high into the sky. Its log-shaped cars sat on the track, waiting to be taken for a ride. Hanna could hardly wait as she ran through the empty queue line and started the ride.

Hanna hopped into a car and heard the familiar clickety-clack of the car being pulled up the track. The car climbed higher and higher. There were a few small drops and then—*wham!* The car plummeted straight down. Her stomach dropped and she let out a wild scream. This was too cool!

Hanna was hooked. She rode the log flume again and again.

By the time she noticed that she was shivering, Hanna had lost count of how many times she had ridden Splash Down. It was a chilly night, and her clothes were soaking wet. This time when the cars stopped, Hanna stepped off the ride and promptly sneezed.

"Bless you," said a stern, familiar voice. Hanna yelped and whirled around.

There on the platform stood Mr. and Mrs. Hoot, Hanna's parents! Her father held a map to Cliff Top Coasters in his hand.

"I found this in the copier at The Gag Bag," he said. "It's got your handwriting on it—and a plan dated for tonight. Your mother checked your bed and found it stuffed with pillows—and a tape recorder playing snoring sounds! You've got a lot of explaining to do!"

Hanna sneezed pitifully as her parents dragged her home. They forced her to go to school the next day, even though she wasn't feeling well. Her mother said it was her own fault.

Hanna sat slumped at her desk, sneezing and looking miserable. Not only did she miss out on the chance to see Jake and Carlos scared out of their wits by her pranks, but the boys were bragging all over school.

"We caught the caretaker, Mr. Finley, pretending to haunt the park," Carlos gloated. "George Jagger is calling us heroes. He even said he'd name his next roller coaster after me. But don't worry, Hanna. I'll let you ride it!"

Hanna groaned and blew her nose.

THE END

• • • • • • • • •

Hanna ignored her growling stomach. No way was she leaving The Demonator now! From her hiding spot, she saw Jake and Carlos climb into the second car. The boys strapped themselves in.

Then they screamed!

Sitting in the first coaster car was a skeleton in a chauffeur's cap. It turned and looked directly at Jake and Carlos. Its skeletal mouth opened and let out an evil chuckle. Jake and Carlos scrambled to get out of the coaster, but it was too late. A rumble filled the air, and the fiery cars shot off with Jake and Carlos shrieking.

Hanna was doubled up with laughter. The prank was worth all the effort involved in setting it up. She reminded herself that before the night was over, she needed to retrieve the holographic projector she had borrowed from her dad's store, The Gag Bag. It was his most expensive piece of equipment, and if he found it missing, she'd be in big trouble.

Hanna reached into her backpack and got out her night-vision binoculars. Looking through them Hanna spied on Jake and Carlos as the coaster hurled them along. The skeleton driver was gone, because the boys were now out of range of the projector. They hit their first big drop and started screaming again, not from the drop, but from the ghoul that popped out of the car in front of them.

• • • • • • • • •

The Demonator plunged underground and out of Hanna's line of vision. After a few minutes, the ride emerged, and the boys were still screaming. Hanna started to laugh, but then stopped. She could see a strange white figure floating in the air in front of the boys.

Hanna put down her binoculars and frowned. That wasn't one of her pranks!

The ride ended and Jake and Carlos ran off the coaster. They were both shaking. *They don't know what's going on*, Hanna thought. *My pranks weren't the only things scaring them on the coaster. I've got to tell them the truth!*

But if Hanna did tell them, she'd also have to admit that the other scares really *were* her pranks.

Should Hanna tell Jake and Carlos what she saw and admit to her pranks? Or should she keep quiet?

- **If Hanna tells Jake and Carlos what she saw, turn to page 49.**
- **If she doesn't say anything, turn to page 118.**

• • • • • • • •

"Then I think we should ride The Demonator," Jake told Carlos. "We shouldn't let Hanna stop us just because she's bossy."

"Yeah, I guess you're right," Carlos answered. "And it *is* the most awesome coaster in the park. Let's go!"

The boys left the Bumper Cars and hurried over to The Demonator. The bright red-and-orange track of the coaster could be seen even in the dark. Vivid orange flames decorated the cars. The track arched high into the sky and then dropped dramatically. That drop was the scariest part of the entire ride. The riders fell, thinking they were going to crash into the ground. In reality, the cars plunged underground and into total darkness. It was a heart-stopping, pulse-pounding coaster!

Jake started the ride, and he and Carlos sat in the first car. The ride took off. Jake and Carlos cheered, but the first and scariest drop soon had them screaming! The coaster hurtled underground and then shot them back out again, only to climb once more into the sky. Another huge drop awaited them.

Suddenly the car jerked to a quick stop and the cars began to roll backward. Panicked, Jake and Carlos looked at each other. The Demonator was not supposed to go in reverse! They screamed in terror as the coaster plunged back down the steep incline that it had just climbed.

The Demonator hurtled along on its strange backward journey. Again, Jake and Carlos were hurled into the tunnel, this time in reverse. Blackness surrounded them. The boys grew quiet. Then, suddenly, the sound of screams filled the tunnel—but neither Jake or Carlos were screaming!

"How do we stop this thing?" Carlos yelled. But there was nothing they could do.

Finally The Demonator returned to the start of the ride. Jake and Carlos jumped off as fast as they could.

"Something's going on here, Jake," Carlos said. He glanced around fearfully, then he froze. "Look! There's someone by the coaster's control panel!"

A man was bending over the control panel. He held a large black bag in one hand. He looked up when he heard Carlos yell. With a cry of alarm, he ran off into the dark park. In his hurry, he dropped his bag.

Jake and Carlos ran after him. The man disappeared into the shadows. Jake fumbled in his pocket for his flashlight. Turning it on, he swung the beam over the dark rides, but the man was gone.

• • • • • • • • •

"Jake, I know that guy!" Carlos said excitedly. "That was Dr. Jasper!"

Jake gasped. Dr. Jasper was known throughout Riverside for being very odd. Once the scientist wrapped himself from head to toe in aluminum foil and walked around town. When people asked what he was doing, he said he was designing a new thermal winter coat.

"There's no doubt Dr. Jasper has something to do with the strange happenings at Cliff Top Coasters," Jake told Carlos. "Why else would he be here fooling around with the rides? We better keep looking for him, before he gets away."

"Look, we know who he is and where he lives," said Carlos. "Let's go back to The Demonator and get that bag he dropped in case he plans to circle back and retrieve it. There are probably clues in there. We can find out what he's doing here, and it'll be proof that he was here tonight!"

What should Jake and Carlos do?

- **If Jake and Carlos return to The Demonator and look through Dr. Jasper's bag, turn to page 62.**
- **If they continue to search for Dr. Jasper, turn to page 106.**

• • • • • • • •

Her stomach grumbling loudly Hanna slipped out of her hiding spot and headed toward the food court. She shined her flashlight on the deserted pizza, hot dog, and hamburger stands. But everything had been packed up and put away for the night.

Then Hanna spotted a popcorn stand. The popper still had popcorn in it! She walked behind the stand and filled a red-and-white checked box to the top. Digging into her pocket she left a dollar on the countertop.

Munching happily, she walked over to a bench to sit down. But Hanna never made it to the bench.

As she crossed the path, two figures in long black cloaks stepped in front of her. Screaming, Hanna turned and ran, spilling popcorn everywhere. She ran back toward The Demonator, hoping to find the boys. But Jake and Carlos were nowhere to be seen, and the creatures were right behind her, moaning eerily. They chased Hanna into a corner.

As the spooky strangers closed in around her, Hanna could see their strangely glowing faces underneath the hood of their cloaks. Hanna ran right past them and straight out of the park.

Laughing, the cloaked figures removed their hoods. It was Jake and Carlos—with glow-in-the-dark makeup on their faces.

"With Hanna out of the way," Jake said, "we can

find out what is really going on at the park."

Carlos smiled. "It feels good to trick the trickster!"

The next day at school Jake and Carlos were bragging to everyone how they spent the night at Cliff Top Coasters—and tricked Hanna Hoot. Even better, now they were able to explain away the strange happenings at the park.

Just that morning a report from one of George's mechanics had revealed a technical problem with The Demonator. A short circuit was causing the ride to turn on and off by itself. This was the cause of the "haunting," so Cliff Top Coasters was ghost-free!

Hanna scowled as she sat at her desk and listened to everyone talk about the events of last night. She watched as Jake and Carlos gabbed away with two of the most popular girls in school.

"Sure, we'd love to show you around Cliff Top Coasters this afternoon," Carlos said to the girls. Jake was blushing furiously.

Hanna smiled. She reached down and patted her backpack of tricks. Now she knew exactly how to get even with Jake and Carlos!

THE END

• • • • • • • • •

"Okay," Hanna whispered to Jake. "We'll wait, but if he *is* up to something, I'm not letting him get away with it." She took off her backpack and pulled out a compact digital camcorder. As Mr. Finley continued to move around, Hanna began to film him.

The kids watched as Mr. Finley once again went into the shed. This time he came out with a huge spotlight. When he turned it on, the light flashed on and off into the night sky. Smiling at this, Mr. Finley then turned on the stereo. Eerie screams filled the air.

"This park should have been mine," he growled to himself, as he stood right next to where the children were hiding. "My family built this park! It was a dark day when my father had to sell out to the Snoggle family. Snoggle should have sold the park back to me! I'll not have some stranger run it—I'd rather see it go out of business. I'll haunt this park until no one will set foot in it." With that, Mr. Finley stomped back into the shed.

Jake looked at Hanna. "Did you get that on tape?"

Hanna grinned. "The entire thing. I have him turning on the stereo and the light—plus his little confession at the end."

Carlos stood up. "We need to get out of here before he comes back."

• • • • • • • • • • •

Hanna, Jake, and Carlos raced through the park's exit and ran all the way back to Jake's house. At first George wasn't too happy to be woken up, but he was all smiles when Hanna played the tape for him.

"Mr. Snoggle did tell me that Mr. Finley wanted to buy the park," George asked. "But Finley didn't have enough money. I guess I'll call the police and turn the tape over to them as evidence. Thank you so much, guys. I really owe you one."

"Thank Hanna, George," Jake said. "She warned us about Finley—and it was her videotape."

"Thank you, Hanna," George said. "Is there anything I can do to repay you?"

"Now that you mention it, I wouldn't mind helping you plan April Fools' Day at the park," Hanna said with a smile.

THE END

• • • • • • • • • •

"No police, Hanna," Jake said.

He turned to Arnie Drip. "You're coming with us so that you can tell your story to my brother," Jake said. Arnie looked terrified. Jake smiled. "Don't worry—I've got an idea!"

Jake, Carlos, and Hanna left the park with a reluctant Arnie. They made their way to Jake's house and woke up George.

Everyone sat in the living room as Jake explained the night's adventure to George. George was furious, both at Arnie and the kids.

"You never should have gone to the park at night," George told Jake, Carlos, and Hanna. "It's dangerous—the rides are only meant to be ridden with staff supervision. You could have been hurt—or worse."

"As for you, Arnie Drip," George continued. "I don't know what to say. You almost put me out of business."

"But George, Arnie designed The Demonator," Carlos said, his voice filled with admiration. "It's the most intense, jaw-dropping coaster around!"

"I was thinking maybe you could give Arnie a job at Cliff Top Coasters," Jake said.

George looked at Jake in shock. "Are you crazy? After all he's done?"

• • • • • • • • •

"I feel foolish for the way I've acted," Arnie said. "I realize now I should have gotten a job somewhere else and designed the best coaster ever—that would have been a much better revenge on Mr. Snoggle."

"Do you still want to design roller coasters, or do you just want to get even with Mr. Snoggle?" George asked.

"All I want to do is go back to designing coasters. I love it! For months, I've been thinking of this new bobsled coaster—"

George stopped him right there. "Bobsled coaster? *Hmmm.* Maybe we should talk, Arnie."

• • •

A year later, Jake, Hanna, and Carlos attended a special ceremony at Cliff Top Coasters. The guest of honor was Arnie Drip. The new coasters Arnie designed were a big hit. The Roller Coaster Society of America presented an award to Cliff Top Coasters—for the park with the most innovative coasters built that year!

THE END

• • • • • • • • •

Hanna switched on her flashlight and slowly made her way through the graveyard. *This is probably some kind of trick*, Hanna tried to assure herself. The whispers continued, growing closer as Hanna kept moving. Something flew at her head, and Hanna choked on a scream as she ducked down.

"Probably just a bat," she murmured.

The whispers grew louder, and Hanna stopped. It sounded as if they were coming from right in front of her. Turning her flashlight beam onto the ground Hanna saw a strange box sitting there. The box, made from old, cracked wood, looked ancient. On top of the box was a skull and crossbones made out of some kind of metal. The box looked creepy, and Hanna didn't want to touch it.

"Ooooopen the box," the whispers now said. *"Oooopen it."*

Hanna was shaking with fear when an image of Carlos laughing at her popped into her head. Jake and Carlos were probably playing a mean prank on her! *I'll show them I'm not scared*, she thought. She angrily grabbed the box off the ground and began to pry it open with her hands. The lid came free, and Hanna lifted it open and looked inside. Then everything went dark.

• • •

• • • • • • • •

"Hanna! Wake up!"

Hanna groaned as she felt hands shaking her awake.

She opened her eyes to find Jake and Carlos standing above her. Looking around, Hanna could see that she was still in the graveyard. But the box was gone! Hanna remembered the whispers and opening the box, but she couldn't remember what happened afterward. She shivered. Whatever was inside that box had been no joke!

Hanna slowly sat up. Her heart was still pounding in her chest. Jake and Carlos took one look at her and gasped. A strip of Hanna's hair hung down in front of her face. It had turned pure white!

Hanna never could say for sure what happened to her that night—if she'd a supernatural experience or if she had just gotten spooked. But sadly for George, once people heard Hanna's story and saw her hair, no one would set foot in Cliff Top Coasters again. George had to close the park.

THE END

• • • • • • • • •

It would be impossible for Carlos to disappear on the coaster, Jake thought. *I'm letting my imagination run away with me just because I got a little spooked.* He decided to continue on the path. Carlos probably went on to the next coaster.

Jake made his way to the ride's exit. Out of nowhere, something came flying at his head!

Jake spun around. A bat was attacking him! He felt its wings flapping against his head. Jake screamed and flailed his arms around wildly.

Laughing, Hanna stepped out from behind a nearby bush. In her hand was a plastic bat hanging from a string.

"Hanna! I don't have time for this now," Jake said angrily. "Carlos is missing!"

Hanna stopped laughing. "Carlos is missing? Is this a joke?"

Jake glared at her. "You're the one who pulls the jokes around here," he said. "I'm serious—he's disappeared!"

Jake explained how Carlos went for a ride on Monkey Business and never came back.

Hanna pulled out her flashlight. "Let's find him."

Jake and Hanna started walking along the foot-path toward the next coaster. The path ran directly

• • • • • • • • • •

underneath the Monkey Business coaster tracks. They walked steadily but stopped abruptly when their flashlights shone on a lifeless form lying on the ground. It was Carlos!

"Carlos!" Jake yelled.

Carlos sat up and blinked his eyes. He looked groggy.

"Are you okay?" Hanna asked.

"I guess so." He put his hand to his head and grimaced in pain. "But someone—or something—hit me on the head!"

"What happened to you?" Jake asked. "I came back, and you were gone!"

"While I was riding Monkey Business, I saw a light coming from under this section of the track," Carlos said. "When the ride ended, you weren't back yet. So I went to look for myself."

"But who hit you on the head?" Jake asked.

"I don't know," Carlos said. "But I did find where the light was coming from—look!"

Carlos pointed to the dirt next to him. There was a door in the ground! The wooden door blended into the dirt, making it hard to see. But tiny rays of light leaked from the cracks around the opening.

"I bent over to get a closer look and *bam*! Lights out!" Carlos said.

• • • • • • • •

"We should get Carlos to a doctor," Hanna said to Jake. "A blow to the head could be serious."

"I didn't get knocked on the head for nothing. Open the door and find out what's going on!" Carlos said.

Jake hesitated. "We don't know anything about this hidden room—or who's down there. It could be dangerous."

"Whatever we do, I'm calling for help right now." Hanna got her cell phone from her backpack and began to dial. She looked at it and frowned. "No signal. We'll have to go get help."

"I'm fine! Let's open the door and investigate," Carlos whined.

"I don't know," Hanna said uncertainly. "What do you think, Jake—what should we do?"

How should Jake decide?

- **If they open the door, turn to page 37.**
- **If they get help, turn to page 111.**

• • • • • • • •

Hanna slowly walked toward the park's exit. Her conscience, which never usually troubled her when it came to playing practical jokes, was beginning to bother her. She knew how worried Jake was about his brother. But to her, the night had just been an opportunity to pull some pranks.

Lost in her thoughts, Hanna suddenly realized she could hear voices. She looked around and found she was walking past the main pavilion of Cliff Top Coasters. In the center was a beautiful fountain. Standing next to the fountain were a man and woman. Silently, Hanna crept closer.

"Okay, Miss Pearl, that should do it," the man said. He held a wrench in his hand.

"Excellent, Bob," Miss Pearl answered. She wore a lot of makeup and her hair was swept up into a big, curly hairdo. She reached out and grabbed the wrench from Bob. "If all goes according to plan, this will be the last night we'll have to haunt this park," she said with a smile. "Crazy Coasters is done losing business to the new and improved Cliff Top Coasters. With George Jagger out of the way, my park will be number one again!"

Hanna gasped. Miss Pearl had to be Pamela Pearl, who owned Crazy Coasters, an amusement park across the river from Cliff Top!

• • • • • • • • •

"I don't think you have to worry about that, Miss Pearl," Bob said. "Tomorrow, when all the little tykes climb on the Merry-Go-Round for a nice, gentle ride, they'll be spun out of control. That carousel will go around super fast, and the horses are going to go up and down at a demon's pace. The kids will be holding on for dear life."

"And no parent will let their child come to Cliff Top Coasters again," Pamela Pearl added. She slipped the wrench into her pocket. "They'll all come to Crazy Coasters instead," she said with satisfaction.

Hanna snuck away as Pamela Pearl and her henchman continued to talk. As soon as she was out of sight, she reached into her backpack for her cell phone and called the police. Then she called George Jagger.

But how could she keep them there until the police arrived? Hanna got an idea. She ran to the parking lot. Sure enough, one lone van sat in the middle of the empty lot, and its license plates read:

P PEARL

Quickly Hanna let the air out of the front left tire. Then she scrambled behind a tree to hide.

• • • • • • • • •

"Drats!" Hanna heard Pamela Pearl cry out. "Bob, grab the jack out of the van so we can get fix this tire and get out of here!"

Pamela Pearl and Bob were still working on the tire when the police and George Jagger sped into the parking lot.

"Hold it right there!" a police officer called out. Pamela and Bob both froze. The two police officers and George sprang out of their cars. Hanna rushed from her hiding place to stand next to them.

"Is it true you are trying to put me out of business, Pamela?" George demanded.

Pamela and Bob both denied the charge, but Hanna remembered something.

"Look in Pamela Pearl's pocket!" she said.

The policewoman reached in—and pulled out a wrench.

"So what? It's just a wrench," Pamela Pearl sputtered. "It doesn't prove anything!"

Then the policewoman held up a small notebook. Pamela groaned. In the notebook, she had written down her entire plan to put Cliff Top Coasters out of business. It was all the proof the officers needed. They cuffed them both and led them away.

"Thanks, Hanna," George said. "I'm going to have my mechanic check out the Merry-Go-Round.

• • • • • • • •

Then I will have more proof to give to the police. Hey, where are you going?"

"I've got to find Jake and Carlos," Hanna said as she began to run. "And tell them I'm sorry!"

"Sorry for what? Saving Cliff Top Coasters?" George asked.

"No, for something else. But once they hear about this, they just might forgive me!" Hanna said.

THE END

• • • • • • • • •

Carlos and Hanna grabbed Jake by the shoulders and started running. The ghost, seeing them flee, bellowed in rage.

"Stop!" the ghost cried. "Bring back my bones!"

The kids ran as fast as they could, but every time they looked back, it seemed like the ghost was closer than before.

The ghost was almost upon them when they got to the Haunted House.

"Quick!" Hanna yelled. "In here!"

They ran into the house, and up the stairs, and they didn't stop until they got to the attic. Jake slammed the door shut behind them, and Carlos locked it. They froze as they heard footsteps coming up the attic stairs. Then a loud knock rocked the door.

"My bones!" the ghostly voice wailed eerily. "Give them back to me!" The doorknob started to rattle wildly.

Panicked, the kids grabbed a large wardrobe and pushed it in front of the door. Then they stacked boxes in front of the wardrobe and backed away to the other side of the room.

"This isn't going to work. It's a ghost—it'll just float right through!" Jake cried.

"Maybe this ghost is like a vampire," Hanna said

in a shaky voice. "Maybe it has to be invited in!"

Whatever the reason, luckily the ghost did not come into the room. But it did not go away. Carlos, Jake and Hanna spent the night huddled on the floor, listening to the bone-chilling cries of the ghost. When the first rays of sunrise touched the window of the Haunted House, the ghostly voice stopped.

Cautiously, Jake, Hanna, and Carlos moved the boxes and wardrobe from the door. As soon as they moved it, the door flew open!

"What are you doing here?" George Jagger demanded. "Everyone has been worried sick about you three."

Jake, Carlos, and Hanna all started to talk at once. It took awhile for George to calm them all down and to get a straight story out of them.

"You need to get rid of the ghost," Jake finished.

"You scared yourselves silly by coming into the Haunted House at night, and your imaginations went wild," George said. "I know you thought you were helping me, but it was dangerous and foolish to come to the park at night."

The kids tried to convince George that their story about the ghost was true, but he wouldn't listen to them.

• • • • • • • • •

"You are overtired. Go home and go to bed," George said sternly.

George never did believe Jake about the ghost. Strange things continued to happen at the park each night, and fewer and fewer people came to the park. George eventually had to close Cliff Top Coasters.

THE END

• • • • • • • • •

"No, Carlos, let's keep looking," Jake said. "Now that he knows we're onto him, he might disappear forever!"

Jake swung his flashlight beam through the deserted park. A movement in the outer ray of light caught his eye. It was Dr. Jasper!

Jake and Carlos chased him. The boys overtook the man as he was about to run out of the park exit. Leaping into the air, Carlos tackled him. They both rolled on the ground.

Carlos pinned the scientist to the ground.

"I'm Jake Jagger, and this is my brother George's park!" Jake said. "What are you doing here?"

"Ouch! You're hurting me!" Dr. Jasper cried. Carlos loosened his grip on the scientist. He sat up. Carlos kept a tight hold on his arm.

The scientist's glasses shone in the flashlight's beam. He had a bald head with a little fringe of white hair on the sides. Dr. Jasper looked like he was about to cry.

"Let me go! Please!" he begged.

"We're not letting you go until we find out exactly what you're doing here, Dr. Jasper," Jake responded. "We know who you are, and we will call the police. But first we want you to answer our questions. What are you doing here at Cliff Top Coasters?"

"Since you must know, I'll tell you," Dr. Jasper said. "I've come up with a way to end the energy crisis. No more pollution! No more skyrocketing electric bills!"

"What does that have to do with Cliff Top Coasters?" Jake asked.

"Fear, my boy—pure, raw fear!" the scientist answered. "The scary coasters at the park are the best place to collect fear! I've hooked up machines to all the park's scariest rides. When a park guest rides one of these rides, all the fear and excitement they feel is collected in one of my fear collectors." Dr. Jasper chuckled. "Why, the fear from The Demonator alone could power the entire town of Riverside for one day!"

Jake and Carlos looked at each other. This guy really was nuts!

"But why was The Demonator going backward?" Carlos asked.

"To collect the fear, I must turn on the rides every night and run them backward. The stored fear and a few screams are released. I collect them and take them back to my laboratory," Dr. Jasper said.

Carlos laughed. "You've got to be crazy. That

would never work, except maybe in a comic book."

"I can prove it. Come back with me to my laboratory. I'll prove to you that fear is an energy source," the scientist said.

"Let's go!" Carlos said. Still gripping the scientist's arm, he stood up.

"Not so fast, Carlos!" Jake said. "We can't trust him. We need to call the police."

Should Jake and Carlos find out if fear really is an energy source?

- **If Jake and Carlos go to Dr. Jasper's laboratory, turn to page 57.**
- **IIf they tell Dr. Jasper "no way," turn to page 43.**

. . . .

Jake and Carlos can take care of themselves, Hanna thought, as she crept away. Who was she, their baby-sitter?

Besides, there was no reason for all of them to get caught. Clearly Hanna's big fun was all over, so she headed for the exit. As she turned the corner, she bumped right into Mr. Finley, holding Jake and Carlos by the collars of their jackets!

"Another one!" Mr. Finley growled. "You kids are going to be in big trouble. I'm calling the police!"

Mr. Finley herded them along to his house and made them sit down while he phoned the police and then their parents.

"I should have warned you guys," Hanna moaned. "I saw Mr. Finley by The Demonator."

"You saw him and didn't warn us?" Carlos asked. "Hanna, you have ruined our chances of helping George. We're all going to be grounded for years. We'll probably never be allowed to set foot in the park again."

Jake looked at Hanna sadly. "I thought we were friends, Hanna. Now my brother could go out of business—and it's all because of you!"

Jake couldn't have been more right. The

mysterious happenings—and the rumors—continued to haunt the park. Attendance kept dropping, and Cliff Top Coasters went out of business forever.

THE END

“Carlos needs to see a doctor,” Jake said. “We should get help right away. Hanna, run to Mr. Finley’s house. I’ll stay here with Carlos.”

Hanna ran off, and Jake helped Carlos up.

“Let’s hide behind those bushes while we wait,” Jake said, “in case whoever did this to you comes back.”

Jake put an arm around Carlos and helped him over to their hiding place. Just as the boys sat down, the door in the ground swung open.

A small, mousy-looking man emerged from the doorway. He looked around fearfully.

This guy didn’t look scary at all. Jake stood up, and, despite feeling woozy, Carlos staggered to his feet, too.

“Stop right there!” Jake demanded, ready to chase the man if he tried to bolt.

But the frightened man didn’t even try to flee. He turned to Carlos and looked at him apologetically. “I’m sorry for knocking you out,” he said. “When I swung the door open, I accidentally hit you on the head.”

“Who are you?” asked Jake.

“My name is Arnie Drip and I’m a roller coaster designer,” Arnie said nervously, running his hand over his balding head.

• • • • • • • • • •

Jake frowned. "Do you work here?"

"I used to—and I still would if it wasn't for that blasted Mr. Snoggle!" Arnie cried, his voice trembling with emotion. "I designed The Demonator. It won an award a couple years ago for best new coaster. Mr. Snoggle took all the credit for it. He never acknowledged me in any way. And then he fired me! That's why I won't rest until I put Mr. Snoggle out of business!"

"I've got news for you—Mr. Snoggle *is* out of business," Jake said. "My brother, George Jagger, owns Cliff Top Coasters now."

"Mr. Snoggle doesn't own Cliff Top anymore? So I've been haunting the park for nothing?" Arnie cried.

"How could you not know Mr. Snoggle sold the park?" Jake demanded.

"I quit my job and moved out of town after my big fight with Mr. Snoggle. I've only been back for about a month—and I've been in hiding so I could put my plan into action," Arnie explained. "I'm so sorry. Oh, what have I done?"

Just then, Hanna came running.

"I went to Mr. Finley's house, but he's not there," Hanna said, panting hard. She looked at Arnie. "Who's that?"

Jake told Hanna Arnie's story. "We should get the police," Hanna declared. Arnie looked down at the ground.

Jake and Carlos looked at each other. They knew they should take Hanna's advice and call the police. But they couldn't help but feel sorry for Arnie.

What should they do?

- **If they call the police, turn to page 48.**
- **If they decide not to call the police, turn to page 92.**

• • • • • • • •

"Stop right there!" Hanna yelled, leaping out from her hiding space. Jake and Carlos jumped up and tried to pull her back down, but it was too late. Mr. Finley had seen them.

"We've caught you haunting Cliff Top Coasters," Hanna continued. "Now tell us why you are trying to put George out of business!"

"Haunting Cliff Top?" Mr. Finley looked puzzled. "I'm just tending to my garden." He stepped next to the shed and flicked a switch. Fluorescent lights lit up a green garden. "I light my plants at night so they'll grow faster. But the lights have been tripping the fuse—they keep going on and off." As if on cue, the lights turned off.

"Oh yeah?" Hanna said, her hands on her hips. "Then what is the stereo for?"

"Why, it's music for my plants," Mr. Finley said. He bent over and turned the stereo on. A horrible screeching filled the air. It was bagpipes! "The plants really love it; they grow like crazy when I play it," Mr. Finley explained.

Jake sighed. "Well, Mr. Finley, you *have* been haunting the park, even if you didn't mean to. The flashing lights and the weird music—people think it's ghosts!"

"Well, I'll be," Mr. Finley said. "So that's where

• • • • • • • • •

the rumor came from! I never put the two together. I've just been so consumed with growing the biggest pumpkin for this year's Garden Club. Take a look." Mr. Finley walked over to the back of the garden and proudly shone his light onto an enormous pumpkin.

Then he frowned. "Hey," he said, peering at them suspiciously. "What are you kids doing here, anyway? The park shut down hours ago."

"We were trying to find out if the park is really haunted," Carlos told the caretaker.

Mr. Finley looked angry. "Does that give you the right to break into the park? You all are going to be in serious trouble. Jake, I'm calling your brother right now." Mr. Finley stormed off.

Jake glanced at his friends. "Sorry, guys," he said. "Looks like we're going to be in big trouble. But I don't care. Now that we can prove the park isn't haunted, Cliff Top Coasters is saved!"

THE END

• • • • • • • • • •

Checking the map, Jake and Carlos saw that Hanna should be near the Bugging Out ride by now. They ran as fast as they could and found Hanna riding the mini-coaster.

"That was awesome," Hanna said, as she stepped off the ride. "What are you doing here? Scared?"

Jake and Carlos quickly filled her in on Mr. Borley. Then they asked to use her phone.

"Who knew old Boring Borley had it in him?" Hanna said, shaking her head. "We don't need to call for help. I've got a better idea."

Mr. Borley was just about to turn off the boom box and head home when he heard a strange noise coming from behind The Demonator.

A huge, glowing ten-foot figure slowly moved from behind the shadows. It was wrapped in flowing iridescent robes and had the face of a wolf.

"Who's there?" Mr. Borley stammered nervously.

"Silence!" a deep voice thundered. "We are the spirits of Cliff Top Coasters! Why do you disturb us every night?"

"I didn't mean, I mean, I only wanted to—" Mr. Borley stuttered.

"I said silence!" One of the creature's arms

• • • • • • • • •

rose and threw something at Mr. Borley. Flamco danced at Mr. Borley's feet.

"Please, oh please, don't hurt me." Mr. Borley began to cry.

"Leave this place and never return," the creature boomed. "If you ever step foot inside Cliff Top Coasters again, you will be very sorry."

Mr. Borley turned and ran out of the park.

Hanna, Jake, and Carlos collapsed onto the ground. They had been standing on one another's shoulders. Hanna was on top, wearing the wolf mask.

"That was great!" Jake cried. "He'll never come back. But you have to tell me, Hanna—why did you have all these pranks with you?"

"Well," Hanna said, blushing, "I was going to play a few jokes on you," she admitted. "But helping you guys scare Mr. Borley was much more fun!"

THE END

• • • • • • • • •

Hanna stepped out of her hiding spot to walk away. She was not going to say a word to Jake and Carlos. She was probably just imagining things, anyway.

As she turned to go, Jake and Carlos came running from the coaster and bumped right into her.

"What are you doing here?" Carlos asked her. "Jake, I told you that Hanna was behind those pranks!"

Hanna just stood and listened to Carlos and Jake yell at her. She didn't mention anything about the ghostly figure. She knew they wouldn't believe her.

As Jake and Carlos continued to lecture Hanna, a sheer white shape came drifting out of the sky and floated in front of the children. It made a noise that sounded like a giggle, then it slowly flew away.

Jake, Carlos, and Hanna stood frozen. Jake opened his mouth to speak, but no words would come out.

Carlos looked at Hanna. "That's no gag, is it?" Carlos asked.

Hanna shook her head.

Jake found his voice. "Follow that ghost!" he yelled. He ran after the spirit.

They followed the ghost to the Merry-Go-Round. There they found an entire group of ghosts riding the brightly painted carousel! Laughing and singing,

• • • • • • • • •

the ghosts seemed to be having a wonderful time. They were white blobs with no definite shape, except for their heads. Big, round eyes were the only features on their faces.

Jake, Carlos, and Hanna watched, stunned. There were real ghosts at Cliff Top Coasters! The ghosts, noticing the children, waved and smiled at them.

"Come on and play with us," one happy little ghost said.

Jake looked at Hanna and Carlos. "We've come this far," he said. They nodded their agreement, and the kids went on the Merry-Go-Round.

The ghosts loved to have fun and they were very friendly, although they weren't too smart. Jake tried to question them about who they were and why they were there.

"Fun!" the ghosts replied. "We love to have fun!"

Jake, Carlos, and Hanna climbed off the ride and got into a huddle. They needed to discuss this.

"They seem so nice," Hanna said.

"I think they are," said Jake. "And I have a plan. But first I need to talk to George!"

• • •

One month later, Cliff Top Coasters held a grand reopening on Halloween. But the park was not called Cliff Top Coasters anymore—it was now

• • • • • • • • •

called Ghoul Gorge. George had transformed the park into a haunted theme park.

Guests laughed as ghosts sat beside them on The Demonator, flew next to them as they rode The Pirate's Revenge, and playfully chased them through the Hedge Maze.

George watched in amazement as his park filled up with guests eager to come to the haunted amusement park.

"I never even believed in ghosts," George told Jake, Carlos, and Hanna. "And now I have a park filled with them."

"Who knew real ghosts would make the park better than ever?" Jake said.

THE END

Read the next book in the RollerCoaster Tycoon™ Pick Your Path! series!

THE PARK: Kosmos, a brand-new amusement park with an amazing out-of-this-world theme.

THE RUMOR: You know the park workers dressed in the disturbingly *unearthly* looking costumes? Well,they aren't normal people at all. They're aliens.

THE BIG QUESTION: Aliens don't really exist—do they?

You decide!